It was becoming increasingly difficult to bear the moments of scorn or rejection. He had turned coldly away from her only yesterday when she had said something which provoked him. She had watched his retreating back and wondered whether this could really be the same man who had once held and kissed her with such passion. He seemed to have dismissed her from his life and it would be so much easier if she, too, could find the key which locked such moments away beyond accidental discovery. But she couldn't. Too often she found herself recalling those heady moments.

Surely you couldn't go on long, caring for someone who despised you? Holly asked herself. She almost wished she'd never seen the glories of Danfield Court—but that would mean never having known Simon. The odd lurch her heart gave at the idea answered her own question. Even in her thoughts, though, she found herself skirting around that dangerous word, 'love.' And just who did she think she was fooling?

WE HOPE you're enjoying our new addition to our Contemporary Romance series—stories which take a light-hearted look at the Zodiac and show that love can be written in the stars!

Every month you can get to know a different combination of star-crossed lovers, with one story that follows the fortunes of a heroine or hero when they embark on the romance of a lifetime with somebody born under another sign of the Zodiac. This month features a sizzling love-affair between **Capricorn** and **Cancer**.

To find out more fascinating facts about this month's featured star sign, turn to the back pages of this book. . .

ABOUT THIS MONTH'S AUTHOR

Lynn Jacobs is a Taurean. This might make her down-to-earth, practical and naturally sceptical but she has to admit that the Taurean's noted love of luxury, art, music—and good food!—seems to fit her very well. She likes cats and admires their grace and ability to find the most comfortable spot in any home. She stubbornly refuses, however, to admit that she's as obstinate as most Bulls! A Sagittarius ascendant, Lynn suspects, is to blame for a distinctly un-Taurean adventurous streak which has found her wandering around India and Greece and Turkey, or sailing long distances in a small boat. It's all great fun, but she's never sorry to return to the comforts of home—not to mention the occasional luxurious and romantic candlelit dinner for two!

STARS IN THEIR EYES

BY

LYNN JACOBS

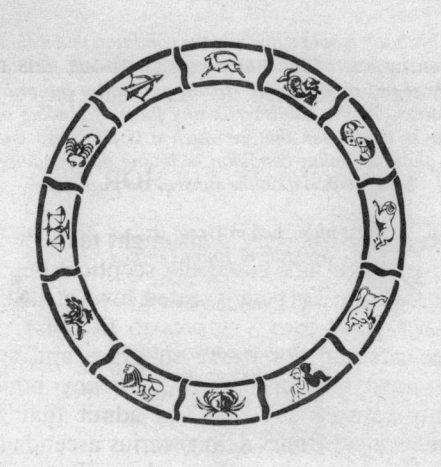

MILLS & BOON LIMITED
ETON HOUSE   18–24 PARADISE ROAD
RICHMOND   SURREY   TW9 1SR

All the characters in this book have no existence outside the imagination of the Author, and have no relation whatsoever to anyone bearing the same name or names. They are not even distantly inspired by any individual known or unknown to the Author, and all the incidents are pure invention.

All Rights Reserved. The text of this publication or any part thereof may not be reproduced or transmitted in any form or by any means, electronic or mechanical, including photocopying, recording, storage in an information retrieval system, or otherwise, without the written permission of the publisher.

This book is sold subject to the condition that it shall not, by way of trade or otherwise, be lent, resold, hired out or otherwise circulated without the prior consent of the publisher in any form of binding or cover other than that in which it is published and without a similar condition including this condition being imposed on the subsequent purchaser.

*First published in Great Britain 1991
by Mills & Boon Limited*

© Lynn Jacobs 1991

*Australian copyright 1991
Philippine copyright 1991
This edition 1991*

ISBN 0 263 77367 1

STARSIGN ROMANCES is a trademark of Harlequin Enterprises B.V., Fribourg Branch. Mills and Boon is an authorised user.

*Set in 10 on 11 pt Linotron Times
01-9112-56392 Z
Typeset in Great Britain by Centracet, Cambridge
Made and printed in Great Britain*

CHAPTER ONE

HOLLY re-read the letter from her younger sister. A slight smile touched one corner of her mouth, lending life and warmth to her usually calm expression. Trust Jenny—in love again and bubbling over with eagerness to tell her sister all about it. She always wanted Holly's advice, and never took it. Holly's smile was indulgent. Jenny would grow up soon, but not too soon, she hoped. It was a good thing the family were such keen letter-writers—Jenny's letter had been enclosed in one from her mother—since she was unable to return to their Yorkshire home as often as she would like, and she missed them all. The job with the estate-management firm in London had excellent prospects, but it was proving quite a contrast with the more relaxed family business in York where she had first begun to learn about running other people's homes.

It was seven years since then, and it seemed like a lifetime. When she had moved to London eighteen months ago she had hardly expected to have sole charge of opening a stately home, however minor, to the public within months of her twenty-fifth birthday. She checked her mental enthusiasm: her appointment had still to be confirmed. She was seeing Mrs Drayton, who owned the house, tomorrow. It was a pity that her decision had come at such short notice; Holly was uncomfortably aware that she knew very little about the family, and only what the more detailed guidebooks had to say about Danfield Court, which had never previously been open to the public. Still, perhaps it was for the best. Had the firm been given more notice someone senior to her would probably have been free to take this job, which could well be the making of her career. If she got it.

Telling herself that there was little more she could do to prepare herself for tomorrow's appointment, Holly refolded the family letter and turned her attention to the meal the waiter had just brought her. She didn't much enjoy eating alone in restaurants—it tended to make her feel conspicuous, and sometimes invited unwanted comments from lone male diners, but she accepted it as an occasional part of the job. Not that there were many other people in the Antelope's dining-room tonight; it was half empty. She had a corner seat, which gave her ample opportunity to observe without being noticed herself. Most of the other diners seemed a mixture of businessmen, presumably staying, like her, in the hotel, and couples who were probably local. It was too early in the year for many tourists, even in a town as attractive as this. Holly hoped the situation would be very different later in the year, once Danfield Court was open to visitors.

A couple were shown to a table not far from hers. More locals, Holly decided as they exchanged greetings with other diners. The woman was tall and blonde, a year or two older than Holly and very much what she had always thought of as the 'County' type: fair complexion, single row of pearls, classically straight nose and an elegance of manner and an air of assurance which made her instantly noticeable. The sort of woman one could just imagine maturing into a gracious, if slightly aloof lady of the manor some twenty years from now. Holly smiled again at her own imaginings, but doubted if she was far wrong. Certainly the *maître d'hôtel* was hurrying to show her every attention. Or was it her? Holly was suddenly less certain that it was the woman who inspired the deferential treatment.

Her partner was tall and very dark, almost swarthy. Definitely *not* 'tall, dark and handsome'. His hair too, was not conventionally disciplined—just a fraction too long. As he shrugged out of his coat and handed it to the attentive waiter, Holly couldn't help noticing the width of his shoulders. Probably the clumsy sort, she thought. But something about the way he held the chair for his companion, and about the way he moved, made her wonder. She could be wrong.

She found herself wondering about them. She could place the woman, but he was much less easily pigeonholed. He was certainly being very polite to his companion, but he wasn't fussing over her. Were they married? No. She couldn't see the woman's left hand, but she seemed to be making too much of an effort to be a wife, Holly decided with a touch of cynicism. Engaged? Possibly, but the man wasn't displaying any of the symptoms which Jenny would emphatically have considered essential in a fiancé. They might, of course, just be friends, but there was an intimacy, particularly in the way the woman constantly leaned towards him as she spoke and touched his hand, that seemed to suggest something else, on her side at least.

Holly was too far away to overhear their conversation, which might have confirmed her speculations. Not that it mattered; it was only the sort of idle musing which she supposed most solitary diners indulged in. A burst of laughter made her look up, smiling involuntarily. It was the unknown man, she realised, his harsh features warmed by sudden amusement, his wide grin revealing white, straight teeth. It transformed him from someone remote, possibly even intimidating, into a far more interesting character. Perhaps the blonde woman's attentions were for more than the man's expensive tailoring and the sense of power that he seemed to generate.

Stop it, Holly told herself, becoming suddenly annoyed with her wandering thoughts. She had no grounds for her ideas, and the couple would rightly be appalled if they knew of them. *She* might believe romance was an illusion, but it was one most people seemed to enjoy, if her sister was any judge, and she had no right to be so sceptical about other people. Holly concentrated on finishing her own meal, and tried to ignore the couple.

Unfortunately, she had to pass close to their table to leave. The dining-room had filled up in the past half-hour, and she found herself brushing close to the blonde woman, accidentally knocking her napkin to the floor. Embarrassed, hating to seem careless, Holy stooped automatically to retrieve it, murmuring an apology. The man's hand was there before her, though she hadn't seen him move. Her fingers brushed his and dropped away. Confused by a sudden and unfamiliar sensation, she snatched her hand back and straightened, her eyes fleetingly meeting his. They were dark brown, and his face held nothing except indifference and mild irritation before he looked dismissively away. Feeling uncharacteristically awkward, Holly repeated her apology and moved quickly towards the door. The woman at the table ignored her. Something about the way the man had looked at her flustered Holly, an unusual feeling which annoyed her. Despite that moment of attractive laughter, she decided he must be as arrogant as she had first thought. He had looked her over in that offhand way, but Holly doubted if he had actually *seen* her. Then she remembered his deceptive speed and the discomfort she had felt under that dark gaze, and was less sure. At least they weren't likely to meet again, and if he did dine at the hotel again while she was there she could make sure she did not pass anywhere near him.

Then she wondered why it mattered. One clumsy gesture on her part was hardly memorable, and she wasn't likely to come across him again. She wasn't usually fanciful, and she was irritated to find herself preoccupied with such a trivial incident. It was time to go over her notes for tomorrow's meeting. They would restore her usual sense of proportion.

Once she was satisfied that she had done all she could to prepare for the next day, she decided that an early night would be a good idea. She would write home tomorrow, when she could tell them all about Danfield Court, though Jenny would doubtless be disappointed to learn that the house was in the hands of an elderly woman rather than some young, glamorous and—naturally—eligible man.

She caught sight of her own reflection in the wardrobe mirror as she turned towards her bed. The cotton nightdress hid the slight curves of her figure, but what was visible was hardly likely to inspire the passion of any bachelor, glamorous or not, whatever her affectionate sister might hope. The face wasn't very special either: wavy, mid-brown, shoulder-length hair swung round her clear complexion. Holly frowned sharply, and her smoky-grey eyes clouded momentarily. She had decided years ago that it would be her brain and not her looks that earned her whatever success she had in life, and so far she had been proved right. She turned her back on the mirror, and went to bed, telling herself firmly to concentrate on the coming day.

Next morning she was shown by a smiling housekeeper into a lovely drawing-room hung with old-rose velvet curtains and Regency-striped wallpaper. The chairs echoed the curtains while the thick pink and fawn Chinese rugs were set off by the oak parquet beneath. A chandelier hung from the elaborate plaster moulding of the ceiling.

From one chair a frail-looking white-haired lady rose to meet her, setting aside the letter she had been reading.

'Holly Fielding?' Her light blue eyes and mild voice seemed friendly enough, and Holly nodded, relaxing fractionally. She mustn't seem too anxious to get this job. Mrs Drayton's smile widened. 'Were you a Christmas baby?'

Well, with a name like hers, it wasn't an unreasonable assumption. 'Boxing Day,' she admitted. Years of 'joint' presents and 'double' celebrations briefly crossed her memory. Whatever other people said, it had too often been more like having no birthday at all. There was nothing special about having a party when everyone else was having one too.

'Good—although I don't suppose you always thought so?' The perception revealed by the comment surprised Holly. This woman was shrewder than she seemed.

'No, I didn't,' she confirmed. 'But why do *you* think it's good?' she couldn't help asking.

'Capricorns are good organisers,' the other woman said firmly, to Holly's utter bewilderment, '*and* they have a sense of responsibility. You're going to need both to do this job properly.' Both amusement and understanding lurked in the faded eyes.

Holly spread her hands in defeat. 'What can I say? But just because you're right about that doesn't mean that you've convinced me about astrology,' she declared.

'I wouldn't expect anything else. But,' and Mrs Drayton tapped the paper in front of her, 'it might mean that you're right for this job. Even though you do seem a little inexperienced. I hadn't expected someone so young.'

Holly had always known this would be the problem. It was her first solo job in a world which demanded experience—and didn't make it particularly easy for you to gain that experience. She was a realist, and had always known she would have to sell herself hard if she was going to get the job she wanted so badly. She had written her CV with great care, stressing all that she had achieved so far, knowing she would also have a favourable recommendation from the firm's managing director. It had never even crossed her mind that her date of birth might be all that was needed to convince Mrs Drayton that she was the right person to take on the task of organising Danfield Court's public opening.

'I'm not that inexperienced,' she protested automatically. 'I've been in estate management since I left school and I've been project assistant on my last two assignments with my present firm.'

'Including Canford Place?' noticed Mrs Drayton, running a finger down the neatly typed pages. 'I spent a day there last year when I was thinking about opening this house. I liked it,' she said positively. 'That was one of the reasons I approached your firm.'

So she wasn't just being judged by her birth sign. Holly found that reassuring, and, if she was going to be judged by past work, then the large Northamptonshire mansion could only help her. Of course, the project director had gained most of the credit for that, but she knew just how much of its undoubted success had been hers. In fact, it had been that which had given her the courage to accept when she had been offered the chance to take on this job. If the owner approved.

'I'm glad you enjoyed it. The house and grounds are

lovely, and of course,' she added ruefully, 'we had plenty of time to get everything organised.'

Mrs Drayton took the point. 'Yes, I know. I seem to be doing everything at short notice. But something tells me that it's right to do it this year, not put it off again.'

More astrology? Holly had to ask herself.

'Besides,' Mrs Drayton went on with an unexpectedly conspiratorial grin, 'by next year Simon might have changed his mind again.'

Simon? 'Your husband?' Holly guessed.

A shadow touched the older woman's face, and was gone. She shook her head. 'No, my husband died several years ago; Simon's my grandson. He works up in London most of the time—accountancy, or something,' she explained vaguely. Holly noticed that there was no reference to Simon's father, but knew better than to ask. 'That's one of the reasons I want to open the Court.' She looked around the big room: french windows to her left opened on to a grey-flagged terrace from which wide steps led down to smooth lawns and the distant glint of spring sunshine on a river. Holly couldn't help thinking of the rather shabbily comfortable and overcrowded home where she had grown up. 'The house is too big for one person,' Mrs Drayton went on, her words unconsciously touching Holly's thoughts, 'and I can't help feeling a little selfish at having it all to myself. Ideally, of course, it needs a family, but that's not going to happen just yet. Although there's Pamela now, of course,' she added almost to herself, her voice trailing away.

Who's Pamela? Holly couldn't help wondering. Then it occurred to her that Mrs Drayton had sounded almost lonely, and was unexpectedly touched by compassion for this woman who seemed so privileged. Was her grandson a disappointment of some sort? Why did he stay away? She had sounded very positive about the chances of his having a family. Was he even married? Perhaps not.

'I think you'll enjoy having the house open,' she said, almost gently. 'It's surprising how much life it does bring into a place and, contrary to what some people fear, it needn't mean you lose your privacy. From what I've seen and read, Danfield Court has a lot to offer and should do well. It helps that it's on a tourist route and within reach of London, of course, but you'd be surprised just how much people really want to visit these slightly smaller houses as well as the great places like Chatsworth or Blenheim. They seem to like the feel of a house that's been lived in.'

'It's certainly been that.' Mrs Drayton's smile looked back into a very distant past. 'A direct ancestor of ours first built a house here on land given to him by Henry VIII in 1537. Probably for something thoroughly disreputable,' she added, chuckling slightly. She looked around the pleasantly proportioned and distinctly eighteenth-century room in which they were sitting. 'It's gone through a few changes since then, of course.'

'Of course. But it seems to have kept the best of several good periods,' Holly pointed out.

'You've looked around?' Mrs Drayton sounded surprised. The house, after all, was still private.

Holly shook her head. 'No, but the first sight of it is quite impressive enough.' She vividly remembered the sense of delight she had felt only an hour ago as she had turned in the lodge gates and begun the drive up the long avenue of beeches which wound gently to the house. 'And one or two things have been written about it, even though it's not well documented,' she added deliberately.

'And you've done your homework.' Mrs Drayton accepted the reminder of Holly's professionalism with more amusement than anything else. She sat back in her chair and looked at the slight figure opposite her. 'Well, we certainly need both advice and enthusiasm, and you seem quite capable of supplying both. I think we're going to get along very well.'

As simple as that? Holly couldn't believe it. 'You mean I've got the job?' Wasn't she interviewing other firms, more experienced candidates?

Apparently not. She had pushed back her chair and was holding out her hand. 'Oh, I think so. Of course, you'll have to meet Simon, since he's actually in charge of the estate, but he's not really going to be much involved with this business, and he trusts my judgement. I'm sure he'll take to you straight away; he's very easy-going. Anyway, this is *my* little project.'

The hand Holly took felt surprisingly firm. She'd make a mistake to dismiss Mrs Drayton as a frail old woman. She might look fragile, but her mind was clearly still strong. Had there been a hint of defiance, though, in that last statement? Surely not. She had made it clear that her grandson was seldom at home. His control of the estate must be confined to its financial side, and he presumably already knew that opening a house like this to the public was going to help with its overheads rather than raise any great profit. It would only be a formality, but she should get his approval soon. It was a surprise to discover that Mrs Drayton was not in sole control of the property. That hadn't been in her briefing notes.

'When can I meet him?' she asked. 'I could get up to London at any time that is convenient,' she offered.

Mrs Drayton startled her. 'What about this afternoon?' She walked towards the door with Holly; she was a slight woman, smaller even than Holly's own five feet four, but she gave an impression of enormous vitality. She must have seen her visitor's surprise. 'He came down last night for a day or two,' she explained.

'He's out this morning, but he should be back at lunchtime, and he said he would like to meet you. I'm sorry it's such short notice, but if you come at three o'clock we can give you some tea.'

It simplified everything. She could always stay another night at the hotel if necessary. 'It's no trouble at all. I'm staying at the Antelope, and I'd love an hour or two just to wander round the town.'

'It's a pleasant place,' Mrs Drayton agreed, adding, '*My* husband and I used to go to the Antelope. Excellent beer, I recall.' The hint of mischief in her voice dispelled Holly's image of a sedate sherry in the lounge bar. She suddenly saw how pretty the other woman must once have been; even now she still had enormous charm.

At ten to three that afternoon Holly was only fifty yards inside the lodge gates when she felt the tell-tale tug on the steering-wheel and the jolting of the car. Oh, no. Not now. It was at least half a mile to the house. Reluctantly, she stopped the car and got out. Yes. The right front tyre was totally flat. She'd ruin the wheel if she tried to drive on it, and she knew there was no one in the lodge to take a message or phone the house, and she *hated* being late. She looked up the empty drive; she hadn't much choice. Opening the rear of the car, she took out the overalls that she carried for such emergencies, the spare wheel and the jack. She had no gloves, but at least the weather was dry. Perhaps she wouldn't look too much of a wreck by the time she got to the interview with this absentee grandson. If she ever did.

Something glinting behind the car caught her eye. Glass. She carefully picked up the fragments of mirror and put them in the car, feeling a rising sense of indignation. What inconsiderate lout had left them lying around like that? They were certain to do damage, either to passing cars like hers or to any animals which might step on them. She looked around. For all she knew there were deer in the grounds. In parkland like this there ought to be. She hoped there were.

She was wasting time, and she had none to spare. Briskly she located the jack under the car and started pumping. It wasn't the first flat tyre she'd changed; she'd long ago given up expecting some Galahad to pull up and offer to help. The wheel-nuts were tight but not impossible, even if one, inevitably, jammed at first so that the wrench slipped in her grasp, bruising her thumb and chipping a nail. Damn. She wasn't going to impress any prospective employer this way.

It didn't take long, but the clock on the tower had struck three some minutes before she was ready to replace the tools and wipe the worst of the dirt from her hands. She cursed as she discovered a run in her tights. She could only hope that Simon Drayton would turn out to be as pleasant and approachable as his grandmother, and wouldn't notice such details.

Kicking the offending wheel as she climbed back into her car, Holly wondered just what he would be like. His grandmother had called him 'easygoing', hadn't she? That could mean anything, even indifference. He might have his grandmother's attractiveness, but those fair good looks could just as easily have produced the sort of chinless and overbred type you might expect from a family as old as theirs. It certainly didn't sound as though he took much interest in the house if he spent most of his time in London. She looked around as she resumed her interrupted progress up the drive; how could anyone who owned something like this bear to live anywhere else? The last of the early spring sunshine flickered through the branches, casting long shadows over lawns and warming a distant brick wall which must enclose a garden. The mellow stone of the house front was also in shadow.

As she approached the front of the house another car swept towards her, gravel scattering beneath its wheels as the driver took the corner far too fast and sped on towards the lodge. Holly had to swerve sharply to avoid it. There had been a touch of temper in the squeal of brakes, she thought, but that didn't excuse such recklessness. She had caught a glimpse of the driver's fair hair, but had had time to see nothing else. With deliberate care she parked her own car and hurried up the short flight of steps to the front door, shivering slightly. The heat had quickly gone from the day. Early March was never warm for long.

The door was already open, but it wasn't the friendly housekeeper who greeted her. This was a tall figure in a dark 'City' suit. She knew him at once. Unfortunately.

'*You're* Miss Fielding?'

The voice was hard, curt, leaving her in no doubt that he had recognised her as immediately as she had identified him. She nodded.

'You're late.'

'I'm sorry, I——' she began.

'No excuses,' the man from the restaurant interrupted. 'This job's going to need someone reliable, whatever my grandmother might think. You'd better come into the library.'

He turned away, the unspoken order for her to follow hanging in the air. All the cheerful confidence which had buoyed her up through lunch and an hour's shopping, not to mention the optimistic phone call to her boss, drained away. She should have known it wouldn't be as easy as it had seemed. She squared her shoulders, bracing herself mentally as well as physically, and followed him into the room he indicated.

It was dimly lit; flickering flames from a fire in the hearth threw his shadow against the dark rows of books which panelled the walls, making him seem taller and more intimidating then ever. Then a light-switch clicked, and she was able to study him clearly. All her earlier imaginings about Mrs Drayton's charming grandson could be consigned to wherever ludicrous fantasies usually went. There was nothing of the blond wimp about his dark and arrogantly masculine figure. He seemed even bigger than she had thought last night, with broad shoulders and long, powerful legs.

'Sit down.'

He pointed towards a glossy brown leather chesterfield, standing for a moment with his back to the fire and staring down at her, every inch the lord of the manor, before folding his long frame into a similarly upholstered chair opposite hers. He was frowning as he looked her over, his jaw unyielding. It was not, Holly decided again, what anyone would call a handsome face. In fact, at the moment, he looked thoroughly menacing. And his grandmother thought he was easy-going?

What was he seeing as he glared at her? An ordinary young woman in a conventional grey suit? Neat. Respectable. Ordinary. That was the image she always seemed to give, and she liked it.

'Well?' he demanded. 'You seem somehow to have convinced my grandmother that you can handle this mad scheme of hers. Now you have to convince me.' He sounded about as yielding and sympathetic as granite, and he clearly hadn't formed any favourable first impression of her.

'Mad scheme?' she objected. 'It's a marvellous idea!'

An impatient sound of something that might have been derisive laughter cut her off. 'It's lunatic. There's no financial need to open the house—I do quite well enough in my own work, and the farm land more than supports itself—and I can't see any other reason for letting hordes of strangers trample over my private home, leaving sticky fingerprints on everything, and litter in every corner of the grounds.' Generations of possessive ancestors seemed to range themselves behind him as he spoke.

'But it won't *be* like that!' Unusually, she found herself stung into a momentary outburst. More calmly, she tried to explain. 'That's what I'm employed for; to enable people to enjoy themselves while valuing what they've seen so they treat it with respect. And not all the house would be open, only the grounds and the main rooms. All the private rooms would remain just that: private.'

The dark eyebrows had relaxed their ferocious frown, but scepticism had replaced anger in the dark eyes. 'That sounds more like a pretty extract from your firm's brochure. I've read your CV, and there didn't seem to be much solid reality about that, either. You're hopelessly inexperienced, and I don't see why Danfield Court should have the bad luck to be nominated for you to make your first freelance mistakes,' he told her bluntly.

Hiding her growing resentment, Holly lifted her chin defiantly. 'And what makes you think I'm going to make mistakes?' she challenged, her voice calm, her hands composed in her lap.

He smiled without humour, showing very white, even teeth. The expression, she decided, could as easily have been a snarl. 'People always do,' he told her with apparent anticipation.

'Yes, they let mindless vandals leave broken glass on their driveway.'

His frown reappeared at her flat words but this time she wasn't going to be interrupted.

'If this house was open to the public your ground staff would have prevented that happening and I wouldn't have had to change a wheel just inside your drive. I might even have arrived here on time!'

If he was taken aback by her accusation the pause was only fractional. Smoothly, without any apparent embarrassment, he admitted, 'I'm afraid that's my responsibility. Some gravel flew up and cracked a wing-mirror, and the glass fell out. I was going to clear it up later.'

'I've already done it,' she told him with some satisfaction. 'If you want the bits, they're in my car.' He must have been driving far too fast if his turn into the driveway had managed to scatter the gravel that violently. That surprised her: he didn't give her the impression of being someone who let his feelings govern his actions. On the contrary.

'No, thanks,' he rejected her ironic offer. 'But naturally I'll pay for your tyre. If you get the job done at the local garage they'll put it on my account. I'll phone them.'

It was the nearest she supposed she would get to an apology, but his careless acceptance of blame only managed to irritate her. There was something about the almost proprietorial gesture which effectively removed any hint of real regret for her inconvenience. 'Thank you,' she acknowledged, 'but at the moment I'm more interested in what I tell my managing director about this job.'

He gestured with one hand. 'My original objection still stands. I don't particularly want my home open to the public, but if the place has to go on display *you* haven't the experience to organise it. I want it done properly by someone who won't, whatever their intentions, turn it into some sort of grotesque theme park or novelty museum.'

'But that's just what I won't do!' Holly protested, her professionalism stung. 'This house sells itself—all it needs is the organisation. And that has to be set up quickly. It's only six weeks until Easter, which ought to be the opening weekend if you're going to make any sort of success of the venture, and you aren't going to find many firms willing to take on even somewhere as attractive as this at such short notice. Normally the planning starts at least a year in advance.' She shot him a quick glance from clear grey eyes. 'Or is that what you were hoping; that no one would be willing to take on the job and you could put it off for another year?'

A rueful smile acknowledged the shrewdness of her guess. It was surprising how much that hint of humour softened his rather harsh features: it didn't last.

'The thought had crossed my mind,' he admitted. 'Unfortunately, my grandmother has a tendency to get her own way about things. At the moment, that would seem to be you.' Dark brown eyes scanned her without enthusiasm. Annoyingly, she found herself uncomfortable under that dispassionate gaze, and shifted uneasily. Idiot, she told herself, he's not seeing *you*, he's seeing a problem. His next words confirmed the depressing thought. 'How old are you?' he asked abruptly. There was nothing at all personal in the cool voice, which was obviously more used to giving than taking orders.

'Twenty-five.' She looked younger, she knew. That was why she wore businesslike suits and tried to maintain a detached manner, but her slight figure sometimes made her feel gauche among sophisticates of her own age. 'I've been in this business for seven years,' she added, as she saw him add her youth to the idea of her inexperience in the scales against her.

He raised an eyebrow. 'An unusual career choice for an eighteen-year-old,' he commented.

Somehow, uncharacteristically, she found herself explaining. 'It wasn't a career choice, really. I'd been going to go to university to read history, but that fell through. Since I'd done a typing course, and a local estate-management firm in York was advertising for a secretary, it seemed like a good idea.' And she would never cease to be grateful to her employer for seeing her interest and encouraging her to move from the secretarial side of the firm to her present work. 'I moved to London eighteen months ago,' she finished.

Simon Drayton seemed more interested in what she had left unsaid. 'Failed your A levels, did you?' The tone was provocative.

'No.' She didn't intend to explain about the family's financial crisis which had changed her life. 'I just wanted to point out that I do know what I'm doing,' she told him flatly.

'So you say.'

His voice was as cool as hers, but she said nothing. She wasn't going to get the job, she was going to have to tell her employer that he'd been wrong to trust her with this project, but she certainly wasn't going to give this insufferable man the satisfaction of making her lose her temper.

While she tried hard to cling to her resolve to stay even-tempered, he began to question her about her previous work. At the end of half an hour of merciless interrogation, Holly felt as though he had dissected and judged every action she had ever taken. And she couldn't tell from his face what he thought. There was certainly no sign of yielding in that rather hard expression. She gritted her teeth and said nothing when he seemed to have finished.

He flicked through the papers he had picked up from the small table beside him. Then he looked up. 'Apparently your boss shares your opinion of your ability.' He paused, weighing his opinion. When he spoke, his voice was decisive but without warmth. 'I know something of his reputation, so you might, just *might*,' he stressed with heavy emphasis, 'not be the disaster I fear. I'll give you a trial, since Grandma seems so set on you, even if I can't imagine why,' he added without any enthusiasm.

Hardly believing the implications of what he had just said, she felt the corners of her mouth lift in an involuntary smile. 'I think it had something to do with being born under the sign of Capricorn,' she admitted honestly.

He buried his head in both hands and groaned before looking back up at her, a touch of humour briefly warming his face once more. 'The lunatic thing is, I believe you,' he sighed. 'I hate to ask this, but do you share her superstitions?'

'Certainly not.'

'Thank heaven for that. At least I won't have to cope with two people who think everything can be sorted out by judicious reference to tea leaves,' he said with what sounded like genuine relief. Then his voice was stern again. 'All right, Miss Fielding. I'll take the risk. But I still think the whole venture's misguided, and that you haven't the experience to cope with it. If I see a single thing I don't like, I won't hesitate to break whatever contract we exchange, and I'll make sure that my right to do so is written into it.'

'But I thought——' Holly began, only to be interrupted.

'Thought what?'

'Your grandmother said you spent most of your time in London,' she explained, 'so I don't see how you can oversee——'

Infuriatingly, he broke in again, the quiet fury in his voice more theatening than any shout. 'In fact, you thought you had only an amiable and eccentric old woman and an absentee grandson to cope with, did you? Well, don't make the mistake of underestimating my grandmother; she's far more acute than most people begin to suspect, until it's too late.' A very private smile momentarily softened his features, and was as quickly gone as the dark eyes focused on her again. 'And don't even *think* about underestimating me. If you can do the job; fine. If not. . .' He left the sentence unfinished, but she had no doubt at all that she was on trial and that her judge would prefer that she failed.

Well, she would just have to prove him wrong. She was going to make a success of this job, and make this overbearing man eat his words. She met his challenging gaze with no outward sign of flinching, even if she did feel a moment's uncertainty. Not only was he a lot bigger than she was, she also had a feeling that he might be just as stubborn. Absurdly, she found herself wondering what star sign he had been born under: Taurus, perhaps?

'I can do the job,' she said quietly, sounding more confident than she felt. She could sense the scepticism radiating from him. Why did he object so much? From his grandmother's account, he wasn't home often enough for the intrusion of visitors to be much of a problem. Then she remembered his implication that he would stay around at least long enough to supervise her work.

'We'll see,' was all he said, but he was watching her closely, almost as though she hadn't reacted quite as he had expected. If he'd thought she would cave in or lose her temper under attack, he'd been wrong. It had been a long time since she had given in to either of those impulses.

The interview, if that was what it had been, must be

at an end, but he seemed in no rush to leave. Perhaps he was waiting for her to say something. Before she could, however, he spoke again, in a tone she hadn't heard before. It was almost as though her presence had driven him to put a question he couldn't even begin to answer.

'Why on *earth* does she want to do it?' he asked.

Holly wasn't convinced that he was speaking directly to her. His eyes seemed to be looking past her to the darkening window and the spacious grounds beyond. She remembered her earlier conversation with Mrs Drayton, and the fleeting impression which had touched her then.

'Perhaps she's lonely,' she suggested quietly.

'*Lonely*?' It was as if she'd mentioned something too ridiculous even to be laughable. 'The house is never empty. She keeps it full of people. Too full. Whenever I come down I always seem to be interrupting a committee of this or that, or the reunion of something else.'

He obviously knew his grandmother far better than she did, and considered her comment at least stupid and probably presumptuous, but there had been something about the way Mrs Drayton had mentioned family which had touched a chord in Holly, and she wasn't quite convinced she was wrong. A series of committee meetings sounded rather like a way of filling empty time to her. Simon was watching her broodingly. Holly thought he was about to say something else, but the door opened and the subject of their conversation swept in.

'Simon? Haven't you finished with the poor girl yet? Come on, tea's in the small drawing-room.' Mrs Drayton held the door open, and Holly was privately amused to see that Simon rose as quickly in response to the imperious command as she did.

As they sat in the comfortable room Mrs Drayton poured tea.

'So, is everything all sorted out?' Mrs Drayton asked as she passed round a plate of neatly cut sandwiches. Cucumber, of course, Holly realised with a smile. Some things just weren't subject to change. She let Simon answer the question; she wasn't quite sure herself what the answer was, and he seemed to be searching for the right words.

'Let's say that Miss Fielding and I have come to terms,' he said eventually. Observing, Holly was fascinated by how gentle his smile was for his grandmother. She was sure that that remark, spoken to her, would have been heavily ironic; to his grandmother it contained only a touch of self-mocking amusement.

'Good,' she said briskly. 'Now we can really get going. I suppose there's a lot to do?' she asked Holly.

Holly nodded, her mind already busy with a myriad details. 'Masses,' she agreed. 'The sooner we get started the better. I'll talk to my boss tomorrow, spend a couple of days contacting some people we'll need and drawing up a draft outline of some ideas for your approval. I could be back here by Friday.' She hesitated. It was easier if the offer came from the house owner. She had never grown used to inviting herself to stay in someone else's home. Fortunately, Mrs Drayton didn't let her down.

'You'll stay here, of course?' she offered at once.

'Thank you. It'll make things much easier.' Holly agreed, not looking at Simon. She had a feeling he had seen through her hesitation and was privately entertained by her reluctance after her assertive behaviour with him earlier. He probably thought she was just being devious.

'Miss Fielding can have the old gun-room as an office

if she likes,' he suggested. He must have read something in her face, because he smiled slightly. 'No, it's not as grim as it sounds. In fact, it's quite a pretty garden-room. Someone could probably tell you which generation last used it for guns—I can't.'

'After a few weeks here, I expect Miss Fielding will supply the answers herself. No, it's no use,' Mrs Drayton added with sudden impatience, 'I just can't go on calling you that as though you were some sort of elderly spinster governess, especialy not if you're going to be living here. Would you mind if I used your first name? Of course, you must call me Emily.'

How could she refuse? 'I'd be delighted,' she said honestly.

'And you'd better call me Simon,' her grandson agreed resignedly. 'I suspect formality will be lost quite early if you and I disagree about too many things.' It sounded as though he considered the disagreements a foregone conclusion. He turned to the older woman. 'I'll be coming down here for long weekends at least until this business gets under way—or founders,' he added with a touch of grimness.

Was that a glimpse of satisfaction that Holly caught in Mrs Drayton's gentle smile? She couldn't be sure. 'Will you, dear? That will be nice. Pamela will be pleased, too,' she added quietly.

Simon shot his grandmother an odd look. Holly remembered his comment in the library, and wondered just how genuine the vagueness was. She also wondered just how important this unknown Pamela was in the household. But that was none of her business; she had a job to do now, and a long drive ahead of her.

'I'm afraid I really must go,' she said.

'Must you, dear? Well, I'll see you on Friday, then. Holly's coat is in the other room,' she told her grandson, and he went out at once with a faint smile of acceptance, leaving the two women alone together. Mrs Drayton's expression was faintly conspiratorial. 'He only gets fussy about business,' she said as though something needed explaining. 'Underneath it all he's as soft as butter, really,' she confided.

Really? Only if it was straight from the freezer!

'Yes,' continued his grandmother, as though Holly had just said something she agreed with. 'He's a typical Cancer.'

As though that explained everything. Holly was about to nod agreement to whatever fantastical idea was suggested when she remembered her earlier doubts about Mrs Drayton's vagueness. 'I don't even have the slightest idea *when* that is, never mind what it means,' she admitted honestly.

There was definite approval in the nod the older woman gave her. 'Early July,' she was told. 'Wait here a moment.'

Holly found herself waiting beside the large front door as Mrs Drayton disappeared through yet another doorway. The house seemed to be a maze. No sooner had someone left through one door than someone else appeared through another. She took the coat that Simon held for her.

'Now what's up?' he asked, registering his grandmother's absence.

'I don't know. I'm waiting to find out.' She was beginning to see what Simon meant about his grandmother getting her own way.

Mrs Drayton emerged from the other room, holding something wrapped in brown paper. She offered it to Holly. 'Take this away with you and look at it later. It might help you understand things a little better.'

It felt like a book. A history of the house? It was probably one she'd already seen, but it just might be a private family document. It was certainly a thoughtful gesture. 'Thank you,' she said, slipping the wrapped book into the neat black case she carried.

It was only much later, after the long drive back to the suburbs of South London and back in the privacy of her own flat, that she remembered the book. Yawning and ready for bed, she decided that she might as well have a look at it—the worst it could do was send her to sleep. She reached for her case and unwrapped the brown paper. Then she laughed aloud. What she was holding in her hands was an old-fashioned, dog-eared book about astrology!

CHAPTER TWO

THREE days of frantic work, alerting the team of specialists who might be needed for advice, repairs and general help, and making notes of what she hoped to achieve in the next six weeks, left Holly tired and satisfied. She looked at the neat assembly of files she had brought home from the office and decided that no one, not even Simon Drayton, could accuse her of not doing her job properly.

Her own small flat was as neat as the files. No one really admired a good organiser, she had learned. Most seemed to prefer the sort who lived in a permanent clutter and somehow managed to produce results at the last minute. Well, she couldn't walk that kind of tightrope. And she wouldn't be at all surprised to discover that a lot of the 'last-minute' show-offs did far more planning than they would ever admit. Or else they had very good secretaries, she reflected, remembering some of the messes she had once had to untangle only to see someone else receive all the congratulations. Jenny might keep telling her that she ought to think of settling down and getting married, but her sister had never been career-orientated as she was.

And it didn't look as though she would ever have to be, Holly recollected wryly, thinking of her latest letter. She herself had long since decided what direction her life was likely to take, and the opening of Danfield Court just might be the opportunity which might lead to an important promotion. If she did it well, which presumably meant to Simon Drayton's satisfaction.

She picked up the book which Emily Drayton had given her, and eyed it thoughtfully as she packed for the next day's journey to the country. She hadn't imagined so much could be written, with such apparent conviction, about something so evidently absurd. Of course, curiosity had made her dip into it, but she had been too tired that first night to do more than glance at what seemed like several chapters of her own star sign, and too busy to waste time with it since. She tucked the book into a corner of her case—Emily was bound to want to talk about it one evening.

Packing didn't take long. Her wardrobe wasn't large, and she'd always found it easy to choose a selection of clothes that mixed well and suited most occasions. It wasn't as though she wanted to stand out in the crowd. Nor was there much chance of it. Still, she hadn't done so badly with her life. The apartment was small but well-furnished, and next year she would be able to afford a new car. Not much from some people's point of view—she thought briefly of Simon Drayton's spacious home—but more than she had once dreamed of.

She had almost finished packing when the telephone rang.

'Yes?'

'Holly Fielding? This is Simon Drayton.' She had recognised the brisk voice at once. What on earth did he want? 'Are you going down to the Court tomorrow?'

'Yes, of course.' That's what she'd said she'd do, wasn't it?

'Good. Would you do me a favour? As you know, I want to go over your plans with you this weekend, but I'm afraid my car's in dock at the moment. Could you possibly give me a lift?' The request was businesslike and curt rather than friendly.

It was ridiculous to be uncomfortable at the thought of a two-hour drive with the man. Just because he wasn't keen on what she was doing didn't mean he was going to assault her. Even if 'not keen' was something of an understatement. Anyway, with any luck he was probably reconciled to the situation by now, she thought with her usual optimism.

'Holly?' The impatient tone told her she had been wool-gathering.

'Yes. Of course I'll give you a lift. When and where should I pick you up?' She tried to sound as efficient as he had.

'From my office. Around two o'clock, if that suits you.' She wondered briefly what he would say if it didn't, while he went on to give her directions to a City address. She didn't much like driving in central London, but at least they'd be away before the worst of the weekend rush began.

When she pulled up outside the glass and steel of the modern office-block, Holly remembered Emily's description of her grandson as an 'accountant'. He wasn't. He was a stockbroker, and even Holly, who knew little of that world, had recognised the firm's name when he'd given it. She asked for him by name, and the receptionist immediately looked more alert. Reaching for the phone and passing a quick message, she got up and offered Holly coffee and a comfortable chair.

'Mr Drayton said you were expected. I'm sure he'll be with you soon,' she assured her.

'Thank you.' Mr Drayton was clearly held in considerable respect here, Holly decided, picking up the firm's glossy prospectus from a table beside her. She raised her eyebrows as she read its title page. So Simon Drayton was a director? Reluctantly impressed, she leafed through the booklet before setting it aside to look around her. High technology and expensively sophisticated decoration contrasted with the comfortable furnishing, glossy-foliaged plants and flickering mechanical displays which she glimpsed in a large open-plan office behind glass doors.

Another door swung open and a man hurried out, looking anxious. Before he shut it softly behind him Holly heard a familiar voice, not raised but carrying clearly. 'And this time I want it done right.' The look on the man's face made her wonder whether Simon had just issued a final warning.

A minute later Simon himself emerged from the office. He was speaking to an attractive, serious-looking woman who was making notes. 'Yes, Mr Drayton. At once,' was all she said before turning away.

Simon obviously didn't expect any other response. His, 'Thank you,' was politely dismissive as he saw Holly and strode purposefully towards her. She stood, collecting her briefcase.

'Sorry if I've kept you waiting,' he said without sounding particularly apologetic.

'You haven't. The car's just outside.' She turned towards the door with him. Clearly, he didn't have any time to waste, and she could be businesslike too.

'Good. Let's go.'

They didn't speak much until they were clear of London and heading west. His quietness didn't disturb her at first, she was too busy with the traffic, but eventually she began to feel she ought to be making some sort of conversation.

'Isn't it going to be very awkward for you, having to spend so much time away from town?' she wondered aloud, remembering his determination to oversee her work.

She sensed rather than saw his shrug. Briefly she wondered what sort of car he drove; he'd made hers feel too small from the moment he'd occupied the passenger-seat.

'Inconvenient,' he admitted. 'But there's always the telephone, and it's not difficult to get to work in an emergency if something comes up that needs my personal attention.' He shot her a glance. 'I'm in the fortunate position of being able to delegate much of my work.'

She remembered the glossy pamphlet. 'So I gathered,' she said drily.

'What about you?' he asked. 'Surely a job like yours must make for a very disrupted social life?'

Another test? she wondered. She dismissed the question. 'Not really. Major jobs like opening a new house are time-consuming, but they're not the bulk of the work involved in this sort of estate management. Most of it can be done from the office with only occasional visits to the place involved.'

'Not this one.' His tone was positive, the quiet voice barely concealing a reminder that he expected total commitment to the job.

'No,' she readily agreed. 'New openings are different.' That should remind him that his wasn't the first house that she'd ever helped prepare for a public opening.

'Every weekend until October? Time off on the occasional mid-week break if you're lucky?' he probed.

'Something like that.' It was only what she expected. With somewhere larger the workload might have been shared, but she'd been left in no doubt that she was in sole control of this one. And, if it took twenty-four hours of every day from now to her next birthday, she wasn't going to let it fail through any negligence of her own.

'Isn't that going to be a bit inconvenient for your family or boyfriend?' he suggested.

Holly felt her hands tighten on the wheel; deliberately she relaxed, not answering until she was sure that her voice would reveal nothing at all. 'There's no problem,' she told him coolly. True enough, her inner mind echoed. There were male colleagues whose company she enjoyed, but no one whom her sister, or Simon Drayton probably, would have considered a 'boyfriend'. She just wasn't the 'falling in love' type.

'What? No outside commitments at all?' The scepticism which interrupted her thoughts was clear again.

Irritated, she managed to seem unruffled. 'I'm a professional and I do my job properly. What I do with my private life is entirely my own concern,' she found herself asserting, a shade more sharply than she had intended.

'A pity. I like to know about the people I work with.' The tone seemed amiable enough, but it wasn't a trap she intended to fall into. Why couldn't this man find something else to talk about? And why on earth did she have to find herself trapped in a small car with him? It might be easier if she turned the conversation back on its originator.

'Won't you find it equally awkward having to keep an eye on me every weekend?' she wondered mildly. 'Perhaps your wife——'

'I'm not married,' he interrupted, his voice more curt and hostile than her assumption justified.

Holly managed to stop herself muttering that she wasn't surprised. He *was* her employer, after all. Her restraint had nothing to do with the sudden anger she sensed he was barely hiding. Nothing at all. And she had no intention of letting him intimidate her, she decided, ignoring the contradictions implied by that unconscious decision.

'It looks as though your social life's going to be as interrupted as mine, then,' she told him cheerfully.

Out of the corner of her eye she saw his quick frown as though, she thought wryly, he hadn't expected the mouse to bite back.

'Who said my social life is confined to London?' he pointed out.

The comment was reasonable enough; the tone was repressive. She remembered his blonde companion. Was she the Pamela his grandmother had mentioned? Or was there a whole queue of women waiting for him? It was all too possible, she reluctantly conceded. And not just because of his money, or Danfield Court. He seemed to carry an aura of power with him; she had seen it in the restaurant, and again in the office today. And there was a very masculine appeal to that sort of power which she'd have to be blind not to have noticed. It tended to antagonise her, but she was unsurprised by its effect on other women.

Well, they'd warned each other off anything personal. That left business. Which was, after all, why they were together on this increasingly uncomfortable car journey.

'Your grandmother said she didn't want the house open every day. Thursday to Monday is quite a common period, if that suits you?' she suggested.

'The only thing that would suit me is not to open it at all,' he reminded her. 'But I suppose it will have to do.'

'It also gives time to close the house during the week to catch up with any work that needs doing,' she added practically.

'Or sort out any crises?' he wondered aloud.

'That too,' she agreed calmly. 'I've had some thoughts about what the house has to offer, and I'll probably have more once I've had a really good look around; but have you an ideas about what might make the house particularly attractive to visitors?' A silly question. He didn't want to attract visitors at all. Just how obstructive was he going to be?

Not very. Yet. Even if he wasn't actively helpful. 'As long as your plans don't include lions or funfairs, I might put up with them,' was all he said.

'No lions,' Holly agreed. Wildlife had never formed part of her plans. 'The house itself is in wonderful condition,' she offered. If she could defuse his resentment with a little soothing flattery, particularly since it was so well-deserved, she was more than willing to do so. But he clearly wasn't so easily manipulated; the compliment certainly fell flat.

'It is now.' Again the 'No Trespassing' sign. It was none of her business, she supposed, and business was the only thing they had in common, after all.

Silence fell again. She didn't want to talk about herself; he clearly wasn't going to talk about the house. Impasse. She was glad when the signpost indicated the turn which led to the small town only a few miles from Danfield Court.

Emily Drayton clearly had none of her grandson's reservations, and welcomed Holly more as a family friend than as an employee. Holly was almost embarrassed by the elderly lady's warmth, but it touched her, too. She tried to tell herself that it was just because it would make it so much easier to get the job done, but she didn't even convince herself. She liked the eccentric old woman, whose mind was clearly as strong as her body seemed fragile.

She had been given a room on the first floor from which she could look down on the sunken lawn which lay below the terrace. Beyond that were what looked like the dark masses of formally clipped box-hedges, with a shaded walk to one side. The still early and cold evenings made it impossible to explore outside that night, but she had had a quick tour of the house, and was beginning to feel almost at home in its spacious grandeur when at last she went to bed.

She lay awake for some time. As a child she had lain awake too, telling herself stories in which she had discovered she was a princess who really belonged in a fairy-tale mansion. Now, whenever she found herself in a situation like this, the old dreams surfaced again, with a wry twist. She could stay in a place like Danfield Court, but she could never belong here. Like the governess in an old story, she didn't even really have a secure place in the household and, when her job was over, would have to leave. She smiled in the darkness. Emily, with her superstitions and benevolent charm, might fit the image of the fairy godmother, but Simon was no one's prince.

She thought about Simon, disturbed to find her mind returning to that social life he had mentioned. He wasn't exactly unattractive, she acknowledged, seeing again those familiar features, as she turned off the light and buried her head in a rather hard pillow.

When, at breakfast, she announced her intention of exploring the grounds, Mrs Drayton was not slow to volunteer Simon's assistance. 'You'll show her around, won't you, dear?'

Simon didn't even try to object. 'I'd be delighted,' he agreed politely, if not with any evidence of enthusiasm.

Holly wasn't, for once, entirely sure of her own feelings. It was certainly a good idea to go round with someone who knew the place well, but she wasn't sure how comfortable it would be to have him as her guide. Someone a little more neutral, a gardener for instance, would be easier. Like Simon, however, she hadn't been offered the choice.

He took her first, not outside, but back into the library where they had first talked. 'You'll understand the layout better if you see the plans first,' he told her brusquely, reaching for a large portfolio and spreading out the drawings it contained on the wide desk.

'But they're amazing!' she couldn't help exclaiming. She had expected a formal blueprint or some modern plan. These were works of art. Drawings, sketches, and architectural plans of the house and grounds from the first Tudor building to its flowering in the seventeenth century before it was two-thirds destroyed in the Civil War were spread out before her. Simon turned them slowly as she took in the pictorial history of the Court.

'We got the house and land back at the Restoration, but no money. Charles II hadn't much to spare, and wasn't known for giving it away. It took more than another fifty years before any serious rebuilding got under way.'

'That's when the front of the house was built,' Holly realised. 'I think it was probably worth waiting for,' she added slowly.

'You could be right.' Simon sounded surprised; she wasn't sure whether it was by her architectural knowledge or her obvious appreciation. He picked up the last, most modern drawings in the folder. 'These are what you really need to understand the grounds as they are now.' He bent closer to point out details.

She heard him as he pointed out kitchen gardens, stables, shrubberies and rose-garden, but, ridiculously, she found herself acutely conscious only of him, his bulk looming behind her, reaching across her shoulder to draw attention to specific areas, and the husky rumble of his voice as he commented on a change that had been made, an area that was neglected. There weren't many of the latter, and Simon clearly had plans for them.

'And that beech-walk leads to the belvedere,' he was

saying. 'It's a bit misty today, so you won't see it at its best unless it clears, but on a good day it's rather special.'

'It must be.' If she was honest, she couldn't truthfully say what she'd just agreed with. But it seemed to satisfy him, because he stepped back, and her constricted breathing eased.

Evidently he hadn't noticed anything unusual about the encounter at all; he simply replaced the portfolio and turned back to her, saying, 'Right, let's go. Have you any boots? You'll probably need them.'

She nodded, her pulse returning to normal. 'They're upstairs. I'll fetch them.'

'Fine. I'll meet you on the terrace. You know the way?'

'Yes.' She had a good idea by now of the house's internal geography. It was like an E without the central bar, two wings reaching back from the wide, north-facing front, enclosing a paved courtyard. The terrace was in front of the east wing, in which her own room was situated. As she pulled out trousers, boots and a waxed jacket from the wardrobe, she glanced out of the window. He was already out there, sitting on the low wall, leaning against one of the pair of great stone urns which marked the short flight of steps down to the lawn. He was staring back at the house, ignoring the view behind him, his expression brooding and unreadable from this distance. Holly turned away, feeling almost as though she had been intruding, and annoyed by her own curiosity. It was the house, she told herself, not the man she was interested in.

He stood up as she arrived, and nodded approval of her sensible clothes. 'Let's go,' was all he said.

They walked across the soft grass of the sunken lawn. 'Did you ever play tennis on this?' she wondered. It was big enough for at least two courts.

'Croquet,' he told her, with a reminiscent smile which faded when he added, 'But I don't think tourists. . .'

'No,' she put in at once. 'I wasn't thinking of that; they'd soon wreck the grass. Although you could do it as a special event,' she realised. 'An Edwardian afternoon, or something?' Her mind began turning over possibilities as she spoke, and she was startled by his sudden laugh. For a moment she couldn't resist smiling back. 'What did I say?' she protested.

'Nothing really, I suppose,' he admitted, still smiling. 'It was just the way you automatically linked my croquet-playing with the Edwardian era. I'm not that old, you know, even if Grandma sometimes makes me feel about to turn prematurely grey.'

She hadn't thought him that old at all. The faint damp had misted the thick dark hair but there was no trace of grey in it that she could see. Like his laugh, it seemed vibrant with life. Her hands clenched in her pockets. What *was* the matter with her? He was just her employer, and not a very friendly one at that.

'I'm sorry,' she muttered, and turned to look at the box-hedges in front of her. At once her self-consciousness vanished in a surge of surprised delight. 'This is wonderful! I didn't know you had a maze here!'

His smile revealed that he appreciated her enthusiasm, which made her look even younger than usual, while the chill of the day had brought unusual colour to her cheeks.

'It's not very big or complicated, but I had fun in it when I was a boy,' he admitted in an unusually gentle voice.

For a moment she thought a shadow touched his rather severe face. How long was it, she wondered, since fun had been a part of his life?

'The visitors are going to love it,' she realised,

visualising the scene without any difficulty. His moment of nostalgia was immediately banished.

'You'd better make sure that someone keeps an eye on it, then,' he warned. 'I don't want to hear about hysterical mothers who've lost their children, *or* to find the children breaking down the hedges.'

'It will be properly supervised, naturally.' She had to grit her teeth to sound calm. Did he have to make his conviction of her incompetence quite so obvious?

With little further comment she allowed him to lead her in a wide circle round the back of the house, a warm brick seventeenth-century contrast with the elegant stonework of the front, past the walled kitchen garden and towards the corner of the west wing. Here the path divided.

'We can either go on round to the front of the house and down the drive, or up to the belvedere. Which do you prefer?' he offered. It evidently didn't matter much to him.

'I'll take the belvedere,' she decided. Simon Drayton might want to bring this tour to an end, but she wanted to see everything, even if it meant putting up with his reluctant companionship. The mist had lifted by now, and there was an early spring clarity to the air as they walked along the paved walk between brown-leafed hedgerows, which would soon show the new green of beech, towards the semi-circular terrace with its stone benches and Italianate sculpture which offered the 'beautiful view' which gave the feature its name.

It deserved it. The ground dropped quickly away to the placid river below, then rose again on the far side into meadows and wooded pasture.

'This is glorious,' Holly declared, leaning on the balustrade. Her eye was drawn along the course of the river as it curved round to open out into the wide lake visible from the front of the house. A small stone building in the distance caught her eye. 'What's that?'

For a moment he seemed startled, as though his eyes had been on something other than the view spread out before them. Then he followed her pointing finger. 'That? It's the old boathouse. It's in a bit of a mess.' His voice was dismissive.

'That's a pity. Do you keep a boat?' It would make a marvellous addition to the house's attractions if they could offer river rides, but something in Simon's expression stopped her from saying so. His earlier good humour seemed to have evaporated with the mist.

'I used to,' he said abruptly, and turned away from the view of the lake.

She shivered.

'You're cold,' he noticed. 'Let's go back to the house. You can't take in everything at once, however efficient you claim to be.'

She ignored that, but silently turned to walk back with him. She wasn't cold, but she could see that he had lost what little warmth he had been feeling. They could always discuss river-trips later; she had plenty of other things to organise.

But she couldn't start just yet. There was a visitor to tea. As she entered the drawing-room that afternoon Emily rose to greet her, and gestured towards an elegant—and familiar—blonde woman who looked up from her teacup as Holly approached.

'Holly, let me introduce you to Pamela Weston. Pamela, this is Holly Fielding, who's helping to organise the opening.'

Cool blue eyes looked Holly over with no sign of recognition. 'Yes, Simon's told me about it.' She spoke to Emily rather than Holly. 'It sounds fascinating.' What *was* fascinating was how much disapproval could be conveyed in so few words. Pamela Weston was clearly on Simon's side. She turned to Holly. 'Do you know this part of the country well?' she asked with cool indifference.

'No, I'm afraid not,' Holly admitted.

It did not take long for her to realise her error, but by then it was too late. In five minutes of apparently charming conversation, Pamela Weston managed to underline the fact—without ever mentioning it—that Holly was an outsider who had the presumption to think that she was somehow qualified to organise Danfield Court. Worse, what she was doing was against all family tradition, about which Pamela had a great deal to say.

When Holly answered questions about other houses she had worked at she was met with a blank, 'How interesting,' and, 'Of course, *our* families always. . .' It did not take much social skill to notice that these comments were designed to remind her that she was only the hired help.

'Our families and the Draytons have been close for years,' Pamela pointed out. 'Simon and I have known each other since we were children. Haven't we, Mrs D.?' she asked Emily for confirmation.

'Yes, indeed. I remember when Simon told you you could only go fishing with him if you brought your own worms,' she agreed amiably. A faint flush stained Pamela's porcelain complexion. It clearly wasn't a cherished memory.

So Emily didn't really like Pamela, Holly realised. That was interesting. She wondered how Simon felt. Even when he joined them for tea she couldn't be sure of the situation. He kissed Pamela's cheek in greeting and took his seat on the sofa beside her, and even seemed to accept, without encouraging, her possessive reminiscences. But the affection displayed seemed distinctly tepid. If this was an affair, it was a very cold-blooded one. Holly even suspected at one point that he was mildly amused by Pamela's proprietorial attitude; what interested her was the fact that he did not discourage it. And she knew enough about him to feel sure that he could have done so without any difficulty. If the reported fishing expedition was anything to go by, he had certainly done so in the past.

'Simon, darling,' Holly overheard her confide, 'I'm afraid I've had a tiny disaster with the car.'

How did one have a 'tiny disaster'? Holly wondered. Simon seemed to be used to it; there was more resignation than annoyance in his reply. 'Again? How bad is it this time?'

It occurred to Holly that Pamela was deliberately showing her that Simon took more care of her than might be expected of someone who was, after all, only a neighbour. She wondered why she was doing it. Surely Simon had already left her in no doubt of his opinion of the person who dared to think she could open his home to the public? He might not be the sort of person who needed any support in his battles, but surely he was glad to receive it? The rest of the conversation was not without interest, either.

Apparently the current damage to the car was 'only a scratch' caused by someone else's careless parking, but Pamela clearly had doubts about the garage's competence. 'You will contact Bates, won't you?' she urged. 'At least he pays attention to you. He took simply ages to fix that stupid wing-mirror the other day.'

The name of the garage owner who had repaired her tyre was clear in Holly's memory. So was the cause of the puncture. She remembered the white car with the fair-haired driver which had swept recklessly past her only a few days ago, and she shot a sharp glance at Simon. He met her accusing stare, but his own was unreadable.

Holly challenged him later that evening. 'You said it was *your* wing-mirror that was broken,' she accused.

'No, I didn't,' he denied calmly, and stopped her when she was about to protest. 'I said it was my responsibility; Pamela was my guest, the incident happened in my home.'

'Perhaps you should get her a chauffeur; it might come cheaper in the long run,' she couldn't help observing.

Something that might have been responsive humour flickered in the brown eyes, but he said, 'And perhaps you should confine your opinions to your own business,' austerely enough to shut her up.

Business was clearly all that he was willing to discuss with her, but at least he hadn't reminded her that he had settled her garage bill, too.

Fortunately, after some close questions he gave his approval for most of the plans she had for the interior of the house. These affected mainly the state rooms, which were not in daily use and, although there was some rearrangement of furniture needed, Simon reluctantly decided he could live with it.

'But make sure you check with me before you even think about slipping in any "added attractions",' he warned. He wasn't going to let her forget who was ultimately in charge.

That feeling of clenched jaws and gritted teeth was becoming all too familiar in conversations with Simon. 'Of course,' Holly muttered, her smile probably looking as artificial as it felt.

It was a pity that so many of their discussions ended in hostility as she fought to gain his acceptance of each phase of the project. The few times he contributed his own ideas, in fact, they were excellent, and over the weekend she had to admit that she would have found it hard to manage without him. He knew everyone, and where everything was, and his knowledge of the house in particular and antiques in general was impressive.

'You'd be rather good at my job,' she admitted one evening after he had managed to sort out a particularly knotty problem.

'Heaven forbid!' He was clearly horrifed by the idea. But that Sunday evening was also one of the rare occasions when they seemed to have established an unspoken truce.

They were sitting together in the small drawing-room, his grandmother having gone early to bed as was her custom, and she had persuaded him to tell her of some of the highlights in the house's history.

'Of course, the family were stubborn Royalists,' he told her as they talked about the near-ruin of the house during the Civil War. 'This was one of the last unfortified houses to be taken. The Drayton of that time certainly put up quite a resistance. Not that it did him much good,' he added with a shrug.

'Was he killed?' Holly asked, moved to sudden pity for the unknown and long-dead Cavalier.

Simon shook his head. 'I don't know. No one does. He disappeared. When Charles II came to the throne it was his brother's family who recovered the property.'

Holly was fascinated. 'How do you mean, he disappeared?' she wondered, intrigued. Firelight flickered over his face. His dark looks would suit a Cavalier wig, she mused, imagining him defending his property against invaders. Was that what he was doing now? she suddenly thought, remembering his continued resistance to the idea of opening the house.

For once he didn't seem to be having any such thoughts. 'Just what I said,' he explained. 'No one saw him from the time the Roundheads took the place. They never claimed to have captured him, and I'm sure they would have done so very publicly if it had been possible. I suspect he died escaping and his body was never identified.' His teeth glinted in a quick smile. 'Of course, there's a pretty story about his being rescued by a young Puritan girl whom he later married, but even if I'm romantic enough to want that to be true I'm realist enough to know that those things just don't happen.'

Holly wanted to believe it, too. 'There must be old records of some sort, surely?'

His smile wasn't as mocking as she'd expected. 'I'm afraid not. I looked myself when I was younger than you are. I'd planned to do a thesis on the great new revelations I discovered in the family archives, but unfortunately, after half suffocating in crumbling manuscripts, even I had to admit that the revelations simply weren't there.'

'You took a history degree?' she asked.

'Yes. Up the road.' Oxford. She should have guessed. It fitted far better with his background, and evident knowledge of the past and his apparent love for the house in which he seldom lived, than the glossy new offices in London.

'Why on earth did you go into the City?' she couldn't help asking.

Something tightened his face. 'Necessity,' he said abruptly.

She should have been warned off by the curt tone, but she wasn't really concentrating, thinking instead of the lives of those who had owned these rooms in the past. 'I'm surprised you didn't marry and settle here to raise the next heir to the estate,' she said with careless lightness. And then she realised that, somehow, she had said something appallingly wrong.

He didn't flare up, but there was a tense whiteness round his mouth, and she heard his knuckles crack on one hand as his fist clenched suddenly. All he said was, 'Your mistake,' but she had no idea at all how to put it right. 'You'd better stick to historical facts and get over your adolescent fantasies,' he added cruelly.

For once in her life she was in a situation with which she *couldn't* cope. All she could do was mutter, 'I'm sorry,' and she doubted whether he even heard her.

'I'm going to bed. Goodnight,' he said without any further comment, and left the room as though he couldn't bear her company any longer.

Stunned, Holly sat in front of the slowly dying fire before making any move. What had she said? Over the past few days they had seemed at times to be approaching easier terms; once or twice he'd even said something that sounded as though he admired her professionalism, even if he still resented her present job. He had certainly accepted the extent of her own historical knowledge, and there was seldom anything patronising in his attitude any more. Now, however, she seemed to have inflamed all the old personal hostility, with no idea why.

Why should it matter? There was nothing, could be nothing, between someone like herself and Simon Drayton. She wasn't from his world, and he wasn't the type of man who attracted her, anyway. How would she know? whispered that insidious inner voice. One utterly misguided romance five years ago hardly made her an expert, and almost the only men she met now were business colleagues. If she knew anything at all about being a career woman, however, it was that business and pleasure did not mix. Simon Drayton might intrigue her, but the feeling clearly wasn't mutual, particularly now, and that was a very good thing in the circumstances.

If she lay awake that night trying to decide how to put things right between them, he didn't seem to have had any such problems. He greeted her at breakfast as though nothing at all had happened the previous evening. He even spoke approvingly of some changes she wanted to make, and agreed that there might be a market for a pamphlet history of the house, highlighting the more colourful members of the Drayton family whose portraits hung in the hall and up the broad stairway.

'Why don't you include the disappearing Cavalier and the Puritan maid?' he suggested.

'Thank you, I might just do that,' she agreed, surprised.

He was returning, by train, to London that morning, and she drove him to the station.

'I'll be back on Friday,' he reminded her as he got out of the car. 'I'll have a look at your plans for the grounds then.'

She had told him this would be her next task, and she knew it wouldn't be easy, but his apparent good humour gave her a surge of confidence. 'If you have any complaints, you can always sack me,' she pointed out to him.

The look he gave her as he bent to retrieve his briefcase was inscrutable. 'Don't worry,' he said. 'I will.'

CHAPTER THREE

EVERYTHING went smoothly that week, except for the occasional visit from Pamela. Emily was not slow to comment on the quiet efficiency of Holly's organisation. It was gratifying to have something noticed which most people seemed to take for granted. She was less pleased, however, to discover that, once again, the credit seemed to go to an accident of birth.

'Capricorns are very practical,' she was told with some complacency. The old lady's light eyes sharpened. 'But you really ought to have more confidence in yourself, dear,' she added. 'You're getting on very well here, I can see that, but are you actually enjoying yourself?'

Holly's rare smile curved her mouth. How could anyone not enjoy working here? 'I'm loving it,' she admitted unreservedly. 'I can feel the history of the place seeping into my bones. I even find myself saying goodnight to the portraits as I go upstairs in the evening. I'm beginning to know them all.'

Emily's, 'That's nice, dear,' made Holly wonder exactly what she was thinking. She was increasingly convinced that the occasional vagueness was a mask for far more acute thoughts. She had a depressing feeling that she had just admitted to something else which confirmed the older woman's faith in the stars.

Simon would be down at the weekend. At least he didn't share his grandmother's superstitions. Then she checked herself. Since when had she started looking forward to seeing Simon? Had she forgotten the warning implied in that not-quite-flippant parting comment?

When, however, Friday afternoon arrived with no sign of him except a phone call to say he would be late, Holly was irrationally disappointed. It wasn't that she was bored—she had no time to be—but she had to admit that his presence enlivened things. She had the feeling that Emily too was also slightly depressed by his absence when he still hadn't arrived by dinnertime.

'I expect he'll turn up early tomorrow,' Holly offered in response to a slightly fretful comment on his non-appearance. 'Something must have come up at work.'

'Yes,' the old woman sighed. 'I suppose I should be glad that he's coming at all. I *am* glad,' she insisted far more positively. 'At least this business has made him remember where his home is.'

Holly shot her a sharp glance. Emily was sitting in an elegant chair, her immaculate clothing belonging to a past generation, her translucent complexion and delicate features unrevealing, and her brain as sharp as a blade. Emily simply did not say such things by accident, and Holly herself was not without curiosity.

'Why should he have forgotten?' she asked. 'He obviously loves the Court.'

The white head nodded. 'Yes, but he's taken to avoiding it in the past few years.' The light eyes seemed to be looking inward, remembering. 'You may have wondered about his parents?' she suggested.

'Sometimes,' Holly admitted. She had seen the portrait of an attractive, rather rakish-looking man with a slightly weak mouth, but she knew nothing else about Simon's father. No one had ever mentioned him until now.

Emily sighed. 'I only had one child: Ralph, Simon's father. He was, I suppose, a little wild, and very restless. My husband——' a flicker of pain crossed the lined face '—died much younger than anyone expected, and we were left with tremendous death-duties to pay. Ralph didn't seem to realise how much of a strain the estate was under, and he just wanted to go on with his jet-set lifestyle, believing that there would always be money coming in to pay for it.'

'And Simon?' Holly prompted, fascinated.

Emily smiled. 'Simon always loved it here, and his parents were quite happy to let him spend most of the holidays with me. Then they died.' She shook her head as though to dismiss something that hurt too much to dwell on. 'It was one of those ridiculous car crashes on an icy road. Nobody's fault, they all said. But Ralph had debts which left the estate nearly bankrupt. Simon had just come down from university, and even he could see that no amount of careful management would make it self-supporting. If we'd sold enough to pay the debts, we'd have been left with a lifeless shell.' Emily's smile was not quite steady as she looked at Holly, her hand tightening slightly on the arm of her chair. 'So Simon knew he had to create capital to sustain the house, and looked round for the best way of making money quickly.'

'It worked,' Holly said quietly, reluctant to disturb the memories.

Emily's voice was tired. 'In a way. He doesn't have to work in London now, but he still goes on driving himself. There have been times when I think that it's almost soured the house for him. It's not been the happiest of places during the past ten years.' Holly thought briefly of Pamela. Someone like her, whose roots were in the same lifestyle, and who certainly valued all that the Court represented, might well seem the ideal partner for him. For a moment she was tempted to ask a leading question, then she remembered Simon's own reaction to a casual remark on a similar subject, and decided that this time it would be tactless to probe.

Emily seemed to shake off the moment of melancholy soon after that, but her story stayed with Holly. So the house's prosperity had been created by Simon? Perhaps that was why he didn't want other people there. It was, in its way, his own achievement. But that didn't explain why he avoided the house himself. She had begun to believe he loved the place, and he clearly *could* make time to come here if he wanted. There was another mystery here, even if it was none of her business.

She was up early next morning. She had grown to love the house in the first light of day, in the calm before all the bustle began, and absorbed her attention in its mass of detail. As she looked at the brickwork of the east wing warming into life under the early spring sun, she felt the house's allure as something almost physical, and remembered what Emily had said about Cancerians liking roots. In private her smile was touched with irony. It seemed that she and Simon had something in common after all—if you could compare the grandeur of the Court with her rambling Yorkshire home.

She was walking on the sunken lawn, her shoes soaked with the early dew, when she heard the car draw up on the gravel of the front carriage sweep. He'd go in through the front door. She had only to wait quietly, and there was no chance at all that he would catch her daydreaming.

It didn't work out quite like that. It seemed that Simon, too, liked to wander in the early morning. She was sitting quietly on one of the broad stone steps when he walked across the lawn towards her. He looks tired, she realised, standing up, awkwardly aware of being the intruder, the unwanted guest in his home.

But he didn't seem to be seeing her like that. A smile touched his face, and he raised a hand in greeting.

'No, don't go away. I'm just stretching my legs and taking what feels like the first breath of clean air in days.' He looked around, an expression of real pleasure softening the harsh features. 'It's good, isn't it?' he said softly.

'Very,' she agreed, sitting back down on the step. He sprawled beside her, apparently indifferent to any damage it might cause to his formal business suit.

'I like this time of day,' he commented quietly, echoing her earlier thoughts. She wasn't at all sure how she felt about this situation, though. The morning had suddenly acquired a tense edge to its mellow gentleness. She felt overshadowed by the figure lounging beside her, acutely aware of his presence, and uncertain whether to go or stay.

Beside her, Simon looked away from his contemplation of the garden, and Holly was conscious of his eyes on her. She was suddenly aware of her freshly washed and unmade-up face and her faded jeans, and wished he'd go back to looking at the view. When he did speak, however, it wasn't about anything personal, and she should have felt relieved.

'Any problems this week?' he wondered.

'I coped,' she replied, smiling slightly.

'I believe you,' he said. 'It probably ought to be your motto,' he added with a lazy chuckle, stretching his long arms and yawning. 'It's been a hell of a week in town. I'm glad I had an excuse to get away this weekend, otherwise I'd probably have been at my desk again this morning.'

'Your grandmother will be pleased to see you,' she offered, not quite sure how you welcomed someone back to his own home. She deliberately didn't mention Pamela. For some reason she didn't want to bring the other woman's much greater claims on his interest into this unexpected moment of harmony.

Brown eyes lingered on her for a moment. 'Will she?' He stood up and reached down a lazy hand. 'Come on, let's go inside and find both Grandma and some breakfast.'

She let him tug her to her feet: it would have been silly to make a fuss about accepting the casual handclasp, but she was sharply aware of the strength in his hand. She felt so small beside him, and it wasn't a feeling she was used to.

'Grandma's enjoying having you down here,' he said carelessly as they walked up the steps together. She looked up, startled and touched. 'She told me how much she likes your company when I phoned yesterday,' he explained. He then added, 'Whatever else comes out of this crazy idea of hers, I'll have to be grateful to you for that.'

Warmed by his generosity, Holly couldn't resist a comment. 'So you still think it's crazy?'

He looked down at her. 'Perhaps not quite as crazy as at first. But the season hasn't started yet, and I still have to approve the rest of your ideas,' he warned.

Not exactly approval, but if he was going to support her after all then their chances of success were considerably better, and she had one less thing to worry about. It was with unexpectedly high spirits that she let him hold the door for her as they entered the house. Suddenly, against all expectations, she seemed to have found something that might even be friendship where she had expected only opposition.

Simon joined her later that morning in the office that had once been a gun-room. She looked up from a heap of paper. He had changed into his country clothes of open-necked shirt and corduroy trousers. The effect was much less remote than the dark suit, and far more disturbing.

'Everything OK?'

'Yes,' he conceded, smiling. How could she ever have found him threatening? 'I'll even admit that I've never seen the house looking better—you've got most of the staff as well as Grandma singing your praises, and yet I'm willing to bet that most of them have worked harder in the past week than they've done in years. How do you do it?' He perched on the edge of her desk, looking down at her work.

'People like a sense of purpose,' she told him. 'I think they're looking forward to being on display, too,' she added.

'Are you?' he wondered.

'Me?' she laughed. 'No. I know I'm doing my job properly when no one notices me doing it.'

'And you like that?'

She wished he weren't sitting so far above her. He had a height advantage anyway, and sitting on her desk, while she craned her neck upwards, he could see every expression on her face unless she very obviously looked away. Which would be just as revealing. Why couldn't he keep talking about the work? Or about other people? She could cope with that.

'Yes,' she found herself replying, as the deep brown eyes waited patiently for an answer.

She pushed her chair back, turning away to reach for a file behind her, and using the movement as an excuse to stand up. 'Here,' she said. 'This is what I've planned for outside. We can use a marquee at first instead of building a tea pavilion, since there's so little time, but there is some other structural work that will need your authorisation. I hope you approve.' For the first time she felt almost confident of his support.

'I've an awful feeling I will,' he said, accepting the

folder and beginning to turn its pages. He nodded approval of her plans for the maze, but hesitated over the children's adventure playground. 'I'm not sure about this.'

She was certain about that one. 'Small children don't want to walk miles, and can easily get bored. If we staff this with a nursery nurse and site it not far from the tea and other facilities, I think a lot of mothers are going to be very grateful.'

'I take your point,' he agreed with a wry smile. 'As long as it's safe.'

She carefully indicated all that she had thought of to prevent any accidents. As far as was possible, and then a little more, she would make sure it was safe. She got on well with children, and her free time at home was often spent helping out in the children's ward of the local hospital. No child would get hurt through her negligence, and she was determined that it wouldn't just be their parents who enjoyed Danfield Court. Beside her, Simon turned a page.

'What's this?' His voice had sharpened, and suddenly the temperature in the room dropped several degrees.

'What? Let me see.'

He thrust the file at her. 'This.' His finger stabbed at the page in front of her. 'These river-trips.'

She was puzzled. Then she thought she saw the trouble. 'I'm not thinking of sea-lions or anything,' she reassured him. 'Just a trip around the lake from the boathouse to that small landing-stage below the belvedere and back again. That's why I wanted the tea and playground down in that area rather than by the house. It's quite straightforward.'

'It certainly is.' His voice was cold. 'River-trips are out. I'm not sanctioning that sort of risk.'

'I know a very experienced boatman, and I've checked on the lake's safety,' she told him quietly. 'We can hire the right sort of boat quite easily, and the returns will more than cover the outlay.' As always when someone presented a major stumbling-block, Holly tried to let cool reason solve the problem. But there was nothing at all cool about Simon's response.

'Damn the outlay. No one goes on the lake. Do I make myself clear?' His voice had risen, and she wanted to back off and get back, somehow, to the mood of only moments ago. She tried to defuse the situation; there was no point in shouting back.

'Very clear,' she agreed calmly, 'but I don't quite understand the problem.'

She thought he was going to rip the offending notes from her file.

'I don't give a damn what you understand or don't. I'm telling you; it's not safe.' He might have been stating a law. 'If people don't want to see the house without risking their necks, then let them stay away. I never liked this scheme in the first place, and this just confirms my doubts. You're more irresponsible than even I thought if you seriously consider this a good idea.'

That hurt. He tossed the file aside, and it clattered from the desk to the floor. Automatically, Holly stooped to retrieve it.

'It's not really dangerous,' she said mildly, risking his anger because it seemed as though there was nothing left to lose, and she wasn't going to give up just because he was shouting at her. Even if she did want to crawl into a corner and hide.

'You know nothing about it!' He was standing too now, his physical presence as threatening as his words were crushing, nothing at all sympathetic in the brooding eyes and heavy frown.

She had never yet let herself be browbeaten, and she wasn't going to give way now, even if it was a fight that seemed lost before it began. Just where the argument would have gone she never found out. The door opened and Pamela Weston walked in.

'What's all the shouting about?' she wondered brightly.

Simon shut the file and put it on the desk. 'Nothing,' he said automatically. 'Just a disagreement about arrangements.'

'Not the first?' Pamela's smile was a little too sweet for Holly's taste, nor did she much care for the look of sympathy she gave Simon. To do him justice, he didn't seem to be responding to it.

'Not quite,' she admitted. 'But I'm sure we'll work things out.' Without you.

From Pamela's raised eyebrows it wasn't hard to deduce that, for her, that simply meant agreeing with whatever Simon wanted. Holly, however, had no intention of abandoning a sound commercial idea without a good reason. Nor did she see any need to discuss it with Pamela.

She didn't think Simon had any intention of doing any such thing, either, but that didn't stop Pamela's strolling towards the desk and picking up the file.

'I don't think——' Holly began, but wasn't allowed to finish.

'Oh, don't be silly. Simon tells me everything.'

The fractional lift of an eyebrow seemed to debate that, but he didn't try to take the file away. He just leaned back against the desk, arms folded, and waited.

A range of expressions crossed Pamela's face as she read Holly's notes. Uncharitably, Holly wondered just how much the blonde girl understood, but it was immediately clear that she understood and shared Simon's objections to the plans for the river.

She looked up, her blue eyes wide and full of concern. 'Oh, Simon, of course you can't possibly chance this.' Holly received a glance that held more scorn than anything else. 'I'm surprised you thought Danfield Court was the sort of place for this type of thing.' An elegantly manicured nail flicked the page dismissively.

'It's exactly the sort of place for it,' Holly stated firmly. 'If the river is out of bounds, people are going to want to know why.' She turned to Simon, ignoring his girlfriend's reaction to her tone. 'I wouldn't mind knowing why myself,' she added. She might not be showing the respect Pamela obviously thought due to her employer, but she did intend to get an answer.

'Well, of course, Laura——' Pamela began, to be overriden sharply by Simon.

'Some years ago a guest drowned while staying here,' he said flatly. The bald, emotionless statement held more force than any more elaborate explanation could have done. If Simon Drayton assumed he was responsible for a visitor's trivial carelessness with a broken mirror, how much more must he have felt for a friend's death? It was at once reason and justification for his reaction to her plans. And who, another part of Holly's mind wondered, was Laura?

Pamela was staring at Simon as though waiting for him to explain further. He didn't need to. Holly took back the file and shut it carefully. Somehow she didn't want a noise to break the charged silence which had followed Simon's words. Then she realised there was something she had to say.

'I'm sorry.' She meant it. 'Of course I'll drop the idea entirely.'

'Of course.' Pamela smiled, evidently satisfied with the victory. She turned to Simon. 'Are you going to take me to lunch? I've booked a table at the new place.'

She doesn't even feel the emotions hanging in the

atmosphere, Holly realised. As far as Pamela was concerned, the incident was closed. One look at Simon, however, who had hardly moved, should have told her that he still hadn't left the memories which her plans for the river had revived. His face might have been carved from stone.

'I'll be along in a moment,' he said, still leaning against the desk, his apparently relaxed posture in flat contradiction to the tension emanating from him. 'I'd like a few more words with Holly.'

Pamela giggled, there was no other word for it. 'Don't be too brutal,' she told him. 'After all, the poor girl's only trying to earn her living. I'll go and have a word with your grandmother.'

The 'poor girl' felt her jaw tighten as the other woman left the room. Perhaps Pamela might have developed some sense of her own if *she* had ever had to earn her own living. As the door closed behind her, Holly turned back to Simon, who had straightened and picked up the file.

He walked over to the window, staring across at the distant glimmer of the lake before looking down again at her notes. She wasn't sure what to say. The anger had clearly gone, but he seemed more remote and implacable than ever. She wanted to reach out and touch those broad shoulders, to offer something— apology, sympathy—to make up for her blunder, but it was as though he had retreated behind a wall of glass.

Finally he sighed and turned back towards her. With the sunlight behind him he was a dark silhouette, his face and feelings unreadable.

'Just how important did you think this river business was?' he asked without inflexion.

'It's all right,' she assured him. 'It's not essential.'

'That's not what I asked.' Annoyance, almost welcome because it was so familiar, edged his hard voice. 'How important was it?'

'Honestly?' Holly queried, uncertain.

'What else? You haven't hesitated to give your opinions up to now, after all,' he reminded her drily.

Yes, but this was a little different. Still, he *had* asked. 'I can scrap it if I have to,' she admitted, 'but I think it's an attraction which will make a great difference to the Court's appeal. It's not a gimmick; it fits in well with everything that's here, and a wide range of people would enjoy it,' she explained.

In fact, she'd just told him how he could sabotage her plans to make a success of this job, she realised. But somehow she didn't think that that was what was in his mind. She hesitated, then added, 'It might also be safer to have something organised on the lake rather than just leaving people to wander unrestricted around it. We'd have to organise some security whatever we did.'

When had she stopped thinking of 'I' and started thinking of 'we'? she wondered. But she had known since she met Simon that this project would never be the solo she had once imagined. It surprised her how little she minded.

As he moved away from the window she saw that his brows were knitted. How angry was he?

Not angry at all, it seemed. Controlled. He unclipped her plans from the file, and she expected to see him drop them in the waste-paper basket.

He surprised her again. 'I'll take these. If, and only if, I'm convinced that you've covered all the angles, you can go ahead with the river-trips. And I'll keep an eye on them myself. I'll want to interview whoever you plan to hire to run things and I'll organise the boats myself. Satisfied?' he demanded, his voice harsh.

Astonished, stunned, were nearer the mark. 'Are you sure?' Holly asked, her own doubts obvious.

'It's what you wanted, isn't it?' Since when had that been a consideration?

'Yes, but——' But not if the emotional cost is too high. But she could hardly say that, could she? Not when he was looking at her with that familiar impatient glare. She swallowed. 'Yes,' she managed, a little more firmly, adding, 'Thank you,' in a quiet voice.

He chose to ignore it. 'Right, that's settled,' he said briskly, glancing at his watch. 'I've wasted enough time as it is.'

He left her to a kaleidoscope of thoughts, chief among which were amazement that he had changed his mind and concern in case something unforeseen did go wrong on the water.

Whatever her private doubts, work began quickly down at the old boathouse, and a new motor launch arrived as well as the larger rented boat for the trips themselves. Taking a look in one evening when Simon was in London and the workmen had finished for the day, Holly was astonished to see that a small sailing dinghy and a rowing-boat that she had assumed were discarded wrecks had also been refurbished. She put a tentative question to Emily that evening.

'Yes, dear. It sometimes seemed as though Simon spent as much time on the water as ashore when he was younger. It was only after the accident——' She didn't finish the sentence, but Holly nodded her understanding, feeling the prickle of sympathetic tears in her own eyes.

Simon's decision to allow the river-trips became even more astonishing a few days later. He was away, and Pamela paid one of her regular visits. When he was present Holly sometimes thought the other woman lived in the house; her intentions towards him could hardly have been more evident. Towards Holly, she was considerably less enthusiastic. She had made it clear, without ever saying so directly, that she did not approve either of her job or of the way in which Emily treated her as one of the family.

It was a surprise, then, when Pamela came into the office and said, 'You look as though you need a break.' She gestured at the litter of paperwork spread over the large desk. 'Why don't you come out for a pub lunch with me?'

Holly was suspicious. Pamela didn't like her, and she wasn't particularly enthusiastic about the other woman herself, but she would rather be friends than otherwise. And she *was* beginning to feel snowed under with details. She straightened, easing the tense muscles of her neck.

'Thank you,' she smiled. 'That sounds like an excellent idea.'

Half an hour later she was less certain. Pamela clearly had something to say and was only looking for an opportunity to say it. Holly saw no point in delaying things.

'Was there something specific you wanted to see me about?' she asked.

Pamela was obviously unused to such bluntness, and coloured slightly. 'Yes,' she admitted eventually. 'It's about Simon.'

'Simon?' Holly queried. 'A message from him?' She wondered why he couldn't have just telephoned her, but Pamela was shaking her head impatiently.

'No, of course not. It's just that. . .' She looked down at her hands as though embarrassed, but there was little confusion in the eyes which met Holly's. 'No. I just thought I ought to make our relationship clear.'

'Why?' Surprise prevented her from phrasing it more politely. Pamela seemed taken aback.

'Well,' she began delicately, 'it's just that, with you working at the Court all the time, and Simon being there so often. . .' She trailed off, evidently considering her message delivered.

Holly had never been warned off someone before. She wasn't quite sure whether she felt more amused or outraged. It wasn't, after all, as though she were some sort of *femme fatale*. It wasn't as though Simon even *liked* her, either. She pulled her astonished thoughts together. The woman must be hopelessly insecure. 'I'm just there to do a job, Pamela,' she pointed out. 'Simon's my employer, that's all.' She felt rather proud of that tone of quiet reason; the indignation just might surface later.

Pamela didn't seem quite convinced. 'It's just that he *is* very eligible,' she insisted.

'Is he?' Holly wondered, blandly innocent. A rich landowner with an old name and a powerful City reputation; who was she fooling? Not Pamela.

'You know he is,' she snapped. 'But you needn't think he's interested in you. I've known him for years; in fact I expect we'll be announcing our engagement this summer.'

If she expected her companion to look impressed, she was disappointed. Holly had been fairly sure of Pamela's intentions for a long time. It surprised her that she felt that odd pang of disappointment in Simon for being involved in what seemed to be an arrangement as much of convenience as of passion, but her main feeling was curiosity about why there had been no announcement yet. Simon wasn't exactly indecisive, and Pamela wasn't holding back. It might not be one of the world's great romances, but everyone seemed to take the match for granted, even Emily.

Pamela's hostility was in the open now. 'Your blunder over those river-trips didn't do you any good, either.' There was an unpleasant touch of triumph in her words.

'The river-trips are going ahead.' Holly felt that her distinctly satisfied smile was justified in the circumstances. The effect on Pamela was all she had hoped.

'But that's awful!' she exclaimed. 'He hasn't been on the river since Laura drowned!'

'Perhaps he's decided that it's time he did,' Holly suggested. And then, because she couldn't help herself, she asked, 'Who was Laura?'

Pamela's glare was cold with dislike, and Holly had the odd feeling that it was an emotion shared almost equally between herself and the dead girl. 'Laura was Simon's fiancée,' she admitted reluctantly.

All Holly's ready answers died unspoken. No wonder he had been so angry at her plans. She couldn't begin to contemplate the struggle he must have had in those minutes before he'd changed his mind. She didn't know why he had done it, but it must have taken more courage than she could imagine. She glanced over at Pamela, who was looking defensive. Unexpectedly, Holly felt a moment of pity. It couldn't be easy to be second best, and it clearly mattered enormously to her that Simon should declare his interest. She might not be in love as Jenny would define it, but there was no doubt that she intended to marry Simon if she could. And Simon didn't seem to be making any effort to discourage her.

Somehow, the rest of that lunch dragged past. Pamela was clearly as relieved as Holly when she decided to get back to work. Not that she did much at first. Staring down at the papers on the desk, she wondered just how much the death of Laura contributed to Simon's present aloof personality. It certainly explained why he avoided the house, and it also accounted for his reaction to her careless mention of families the other night. Evidently the wound was still raw.

Pressure of work stopped her brooding. As the opening drew nearer, she began to feel as though she was juggling too many balls in the air and was heading for certain disaster. Everyone around her seemed to want praise, advice or reassurance and, as she tried to dole them out with an even hand, she wondered just who *she* was meant to turn to. Pull yourself together, she told herself, catching the careless moment of self-pity. You know who you've always relied on: you. Besides, she had claimed she could cope. There were times when she wondered whether it was true. She was increasingly nervous, and Emily's blithe confidence was little help.

Good Friday was sunny and the forecast excellent. That means that all the tourists will want to go to the seaside, she decided, depressed. Nevertheless, when the housekeeper made the same suggestion, Holly managed to soothe her and send her away smiling. She herself went to church with the beginning of a bad headache.

That evening she sat in her office going over and over her plans, trying to imagine what could go wrong. The trouble was that her usually placid imagination seemed to have run out of control, and was conjuring up scenes of disaster faster than she could devise solutions.

Next morning was as fine as the forecast had promised. Holly swallowed coffee but decided that not even she could cope with breakfast that day. Unfortunately there was hardly anything to do. The gates opened at two o'clock, everyone knew their jobs—or else it was too late; only she had nothing that needed her immediate attention.

By midday the house was in a quiet ferment and

Holly's principal role seemed to be as a soother of nerves. She had found the missing bundle of entry tickets, moved the car-park signs so that traffic was no longer directed into the river, and assured the cook that not only had she cooked enough cakes and scones, but that there was a freezerful ready in case of disasters. When the gates opened, everyone was smiling and relaxed and Holly was so tense that she wanted to scream.

Simon had been in evidence all day. He was doing nothing to undermine her, but neither did his presence do much to help her nerves. Unreasonably, she wished he'd stayed in London. She wished *she'd* stayed in London. Or Yorkshire.

Her mind preoccupied with possible disasters, she walked straight into Simon as he rounded a corner with his usual long stride.

'Sorry,' she muttered, pushing herself away from the disturbing contact with hard muscles beneath the soft cotton of his shirt.

Unexpectedly, two strong hands gripped her shoulders, steadying her and cutting off her retreat.

'What's wrong?' He frowned down at her.

Edginess got in the way of her usual serenity. 'I don't know. Yet. It's all going too smoothly,' she admitted. And then, suspiciously, 'Why? What have you discovered?'

Releasing her, he laughed. 'Nothing at all,' he assured her. His laughter faded, and he looked at her with more than a hint of exasperation. 'Do you really think I'm going round laying traps for you? That I *want* today to be failure?'

Uncomfortably, she shook her head. She didn't think *that* exactly, but she was too conscious of his feelings about opening the house. 'No, but——' she began cautiously.

His look of scorn should have withered her. 'You ought to realise by now that I'm the last person who *wants* anything to go wrong. This is *my* house. Remember?'

She remembered all right.

'I might not want it overrun by sightseers, but surely you don't seriously think I want it associated with a disaster?' he demanded severely, almost as though she had disappointed him.

'No, of course not.' Once was enough for him, and the spectre of his dead fiancée flickered between them. 'I'm sorry,' she repeated. 'I suppose I've just got a bad attack of nerves.'

'You?' He looked amazed, then a smile softened his face. 'The competent and indomitable Holly Fielding suffering from nerves?' He shook his head in mock reproach.

He managed to surprise a splutter of laughter out of her. At once she felt better.

'Go for a walk,' he advised. 'The best way to discover what your visitors——' was there a faint emphasis on the pronoun? '—really think about the Court is to listen to what they're saying.'

He was right, and she knew it. 'I think I might do just that,' she agreed.

'Good. We can compare notes later, then, because *I*,' he stressed, 'am going to do exactly the same thing. I'll give you my verdict this evening.'

He walked away, leaving Holly reminded that she was still very much on trial. He might support her today because he did not want his home disgraced, but all his original objections still stood.

CHAPTER FOUR

BY THE time the day ended, Holly knew it had been a success. The house had looked splendid and the spring flowers had added life and colour to the grounds. Every conversation she had heard seemed to reflect pleasure and enthusiasm. From time to time she had glimpsed Simon, presumably making his own survey of opinions. As she saw him striding across the lawns, pausing occasionally to speak to a visitor, she couldn't help thinking how much he looked the part of Lord of the Manor. How many of the tourists had instinctively recognised him as the owner? Quite a few, she suspected.

He might have been looking for flaws in her organisation, but either he found none or he had decided, after all, to give her more time before passing judgement. At any rate, he said little that evening beyond, 'It could have been worse, I suppose.'

The cool verdict was given in passing as he joined Pamela, presumably to take her out to dinner. Holly couldn't stop herself wondering how much of the evening would be spent in deploring what she had done to Danfield Court. But perhaps it was even more likely that they would pass the time in discussing wedding plans. Surely, now that Simon was here so much, they would make it official soon?

By mid-May there had still been no announcement, but at least all was going well with the house, and Holly no longer found herself expecting disaster while trying to maintain a cool façade. There was no need now for Simon to keep an eye on her all the time—even he must be convinced that his grandmother's project was working well. So his continued presence must be due to Pamela. Holly sometimes wondered what arrangements he had come to with the London firm. The odd day or two a week, which was all he now spent in the City, could hardly be enough in such a busy firm. At least the situation delighted Emily; Holly's feelings were more mixed.

He was usually polite when they met and, just occasionally, a frail harmony seemed to operate between them. It had been there when they planned the Edwardian afternoon which she had once, half jokingly, suggested, and it was there sometimes when they sat late at night discussing the house's history. But then a curtain would come down; she would say something personal, he would find some fault with her plans, and he would again be the aloof autocrat who resented her presence.

Living in the same house, however big, as someone like Simon was increasingly difficult, Holly discovered. He had too much energy, too strong a personality for her to remain unaffected. He had only to come unannounced into her office, or appear unexpectedly when she had thought herself absorbed in estate business, for her to be thrown off-balance. She would suddenly become self-conscious, her concentration would falter, and she would struggle to retain her normally effortless composure.

She wasn't a fool. She knew what was wrong with her. She hadn't spent years listening to her younger sister's troubles without learning something about the roller-coaster of emotions. It was just, she thought wryly, that she had never thought it would happen to her. Not that, in the circumstances, it was likely to do her any good. She should have expected it, though. No one had a built-in immunity, and if she hadn't been affected by him it would have been a miracle. His initial hostility, and his occasional friendship, the strength of his personality and the fact that they shared so many common interests had all combined with these idyllic surroundings and the warmth of Emily's hospitality to create a reality that was dangerously close to all her fantasies. But that was all they were: fantasies. In some ways she knew Simon no better than when they had first met. And then there was Pamela, whose intolerance of her was, if anything, growing.

It occurred to her that the best, certainly the most sensible, course for her to take would be to get away. It wasn't impossible. The house was virtually running itself now; she could go back to London and just keep in contact by phone with the occasional visit, preferably when Simon was elsewhere. She could even see what other projects were available; she had rather lost contact with the frenetic life of the office recently. It seemed like another world.

Whatever vague plans she was making didn't stand a chance. Her tentative suggestion to Emily later that afternoon brought a distressed response.

'Oh, no, Holly dear. We couldn't possibly manage without you. You won't really go, will you?'

She sounded genuinely startled and upset, and Holly felt forced to backtrack. 'Not if you really think I'm still needed,' she reassured the other woman. 'It's just that things seem to be going so well that I'm beginning to feel rather unnecessary here. You don't really need me.'

'But we do.' Emily was positive. She gestured almost helplessly and, for once, Holly was sharply reminded of her age. 'Simon can't guarantee to be here all the time, and I haven't the energy to keep track of so many different people and jobs.'

She looked suddenly weary, and Holly realised with

concern that the excitement of the past weeks had taken their toll. And if Holly left her now, Emily would undoubtedly drive herself even harder.

If she hadn't already realised this, Simon would have left her in no doubt. When he came into the room Emily turned to him, getting up with a look of anxiety.

'Holly's talking about going back to London. Can't *you* persuade her that she's still needed here?'

His head turned sharply towards Holly, the quick frown drawing his brows together, his mouth tightening, before he went over to his grandmother, gently easing her back into the chair.

'Don't worry, Grandma. I'm sure Holly knows we want her to stay here. Don't you, Holly?' Steel underlay the apparently friendly question, but Emily's reaction had already made the decision for her.

'Of course. I'll stay as long as you feel I'm needed,' she answered the old lady directly, giving in to her distress rather than the grandson's unspoken pressure.

Emily relaxed, but the issue wasn't over for Holly. Simon confronted her when they were alone together late that evening. As soon as she came into the room and he looked up and said curtly, 'Sit down. I want to talk to you,' she knew what to expect. 'What happened to all that rubbish you talked about commitment?' he demanded harshly. 'The job's hardly begun, and you want to slip off and leave it to an old woman, who'll drive herself into her grave rather than give up something she's wanted for years?'

'No,' Holly denied. 'I'd never have suggested it if I'd known how she'd feel.'

'Then why did you?'

To get away from you. To get away from the dangerous feeling that I belong here. But she couldn't say that. 'Because I'm *not* really needed full-time here while it's running smoothly. It'd save you money if I went back to the office and just came down once a week,' she pointed out, trying to sound reasonable.

'Damn the money!' he retorted. 'You know as well as I do that this whole scheme never had anything to do with money. It was you who said she was lonely—are you going to desert her now? She *likes* you,' he added, as though somehow that angered him.

He could hardly have made his disagreement with that feeling more clear. She had already known it, so why should it hurt so much?

'I've told you, I'm *not* leaving,' Holly repeated, trying not to let her thickened voice betray her feelings. 'And I don't think it was my company she was lonely for,' she added quietly.

He didn't even seem to hear her last comment and there wasn't much else to say. She wasn't going to attempt to defend herself; she'd done nothing wrong. If she couldn't go back to London, then she could always find work to do in her own office. 'Goodnight,' she told him, walking out of the room when he ignored her.

From then on, the atmosphere between herself and Simon was as cool as it had been when they'd first met. They discussed business when they had to, but found little else to talk about, and Holly couldn't help but feel he was watching her suspiciously. She threw herself into her work, and tried to believe that this was the simplest and therefore the best way to cope.

At least the work itself was going well. People seemed to be enjoying the house's strong sense of family tradition, and were fascinated by the story of the Draytons through years of success and near-disaster. Outside, they had been lucky with the weather, and the grounds could seldom have looked lovelier. Even the river-trips were a great success, and Simon had made no further comment about them, though she sensed that he watched them carefully.

She should have known it couldn't last. When it struck, however, the near disaster was wholly unexpected. It was a Sunday and, for once, the day was relatively quiet, the weather slightly cooler than usual with a touch of damp in the air. There had been a couple of coach parties round in the early part of the afternoon, but now most of the trickle of visitors were individuals or families with children. The playground was busy, but not crowded.

Holly had taken to spending a lot of time at the playground. While the older children clambered over the elaborate climbing-frame and swung on ropes with tyres suspended from them, Holly would relieve the nursery nurse and help the smallest children down the slide or gather them round to play games or read them stories. On a day like this the few older children, watched by a slightly bored-looking attendant, seemed cheerfully able to ignore the hint of drizzle in the air, but Holly had gathered the three or four toddlers—whose mothers were taking older children on the river or wanted to visit some part of the grounds too remote for short legs to manage—inside to tell them a story.

She was holding them fascinated with her animated version of a familiar fairy-tale when she heard the sound of raised voices outside.

'But I left him here! I thought this place was meant to be supervised; what were you doing, hiding inside in front of a fire?'

The slightly hysterical edge to the accusing voice told Holly that this wasn't some minor argument. Anyway, if one of the visitors was upset it was her business to sort things out. Quickly bringing her story to an end, she issued the children with crayons and paper and stepped outside.

The young attendant was looking defensive. Confronting him was a woman holding a child firmly by one hand and wearing an expression of mingled fear and anger.

'May I help?' The attendant immediately looked relieved, and the woman turned on Holly.

'You'd better. I left Jamie here for an hour because he wanted to play while I took Marie to look at the house, and now he's gone! I thought you advertised this place as safe!' The girl beside her, who looked about nine years old, seemed ready to burst into tears, and the mother was sounding increasingly desolate. Appalled, Holly didn't blame her—but panic wouldn't help.

She turned to the attendant. 'Go and fetch Mr Drayton.' She didn't question the instinct that made her turn to Simon before anyone else. He knew the grounds better than anyone else, but that was just a rationalisation of an instinctive response. It was a crisis, and they needed him.

Deliberately she calmed herself. 'What was Jamie wearing?' she asked her mother.

It seemed to confuse the woman for a moment. 'Oh, jeans and trainers—you know, what every other seven-year-old boy is wearing,' she replied bitterly, glancing at the other obviously curious and similarly clad youngsters around her.

Marie tugged urgently at her mother's hand. 'And that sweatshirt, Mum. Don't you remember? It's the new one, from that film we saw last night.'

Holly's face cleared. 'That's well remembered!' She smiled at the girl, getting the first tentative signs of a smile in response. 'What did the shirt say? Do you remember what colour it was?'

She was still coaxing a description from both mother and daughter when Simon strode into the playground.

He cast one speaking, furious glance at Holly, but his tone was reassuring as he turned to the distraught mother.

'I'm sure your son will be fine. We've alerted all our staff to look out for him, but is there anywhere special you think he might be likely to go?'

Jamie's mother thought for a moment before shrugging helplessly. 'I don't know. He was enjoying everything until now. We all were.'

It was a backhanded compliment to the success of the Court which Holly could have done without. Quickly she told Simon what Marie had said about the boy's distinctive sweatshirt. He smiled at the girl.

'That's great. Well done. I'm sure we'll find your brother in no time, thanks to your help. You just stay here with Miss Fielding, and I'll go and make sure everyone's doing their best.'

He straightened and went quickly away without sparing Holly more than another glance. It was enough.

Jamie's mother, however, had clearly been comforted by the visit. 'Is he the owner?' she asked. Holly nodded. 'Well, I must say, *he* certainly seems to know what he's doing. He's very impressive, isn't he?'

He certainly is, Holly acknowledged, and turned her attention to confirming the woman's apparent conviction that everything would turn out well now that Simon was involved. Ten minutes later she was proved right.

'Look, Mum! There he is!' Marie shouted, jumping up and pointing.

A small, very grubby boy was entering the playground, his right hand engulfed in Simon's left. Relief almost made Holly's control falter. Simon's head was bent towards Jamie, and then he was swallowed up in the excited chatter of Marie and her mother, and

Holly couldn't read his mood from the one quick look they exchanged.

'Where did you find him?' the mother was demanding.

Simon squatted, ruffling the boy's already tousled hair. 'He's a stowaway, aren't you, Jamie?' He grinned. 'Apparently he changed his mind about not wanting a river ride, and managed to talk some innocent bystander into replacing the ticket he claimed to have "lost". The boatman had no idea he was unaccompanied.'

No wonder they'd been unable to find him. He'd been happily absorbed in the forty-five-minute ride up the river and round the lake while everyone had been frantically scouring the grounds. The expression on his mother's face seemed to promise him a lecture designed to make him regret his impulsive decision, but Holly had a feeling that he might just think that the adventure was worth all the fuss.

She didn't. Her growing confidence in her own organisation had been badly shaken, even though Jamie's mother had recovered quickly once she had been reunited with her son. 'He's always getting into trouble,' she had admitted with affectionate exasperation, and seemed surprised when Holly insisted on refunding her entrance fees. There would be no unpleasant publicity from the incident, and Jamie had never been in any real danger, but that didn't make her much happier.

After waving off the now smiling family, Holly headed slowly back up to the house. A mixture of relief and remembered fear gripped her. It had all ended well, but it could so easily have been different. If Jamie had fallen in the lake; if he had hurt himself; if that wretched attendant——So many ifs, and ultimately the child have been safe all the time. With no thanks to her.

She sat staring at her desk, glad of a few minutes' solitude in which to regain her balance. She wasn't allowed long. Simon's knock didn't wait for an answer as he pushed the door open.

'So this is where you're sulking?' he demanded.

She looked up wearily. She'd known this confrontation was coming, but she wasn't certain she was ready to deal with it.

'Yes,' she agreed. Sulking was probably as good a word as any for her mood.

'Have you thought about what might have happened out there today?' He leaned his hands on the desk and glared at her so that she couldn't avoid the accusation in his eyes. She knew he was being driven by his own nightmares, but that didn't help her cope with his anger.

'I've thought about little else,' she admitted, getting up and walking to the window. She stood there for a moment, staring out unseeing at the crowded grounds, her arms clasped protectively around her waist.

'A child might have been killed,' he reminded her. 'What are you going to do about it? Do you still think this place is safe?'

She gritted her teeth. A headache was beginning to nag behind her eyes, but there was no time to think of it. 'Yes, on the whole, I do think that the Court is as safe as we——' deliberately she corrected herself before he could deny his part in the scheme '—as *I* can make it. And the first thing I'm going to do is sack the student who didn't do his job.' She didn't like dismissing anyone, but this was something that could not be let go with a warning.

'Too late,' he told her flatly. 'I've already done it.'

'You've *what*?' She whirled round to confront him,

her own indignation overcoming other feelings. 'You had no right to do that!'

'I had every right,' he contradicted. 'The boy endangered a child's life on *my* land.' It might have been a personal insult which he was reminded to wipe out.

'But *I* employed him, or had you forgotten that?' From his expression it was more than clear that he had forgotten nothing of the sort. 'He, as well as the accident, was *my* responsibility,' she said emphatically. 'He should have had his dismissal from me.' However much she would have hated doing it.

He shrugged. 'What does it matter? He's out.' His tone was not one with which people argued. Holly was vividly reminded of the anxious-looking man she had seen scuttling from his London office weeks ago. But the issue wasn't that simple, and somehow it was important not to cave in.

'What matters is who is employing these people. Me—or you?' she challenged.

'Perhaps, in the circumstances, it should be me,' he responded coldly.

She had had enough. 'Right. Then you can do the lot,' she told him. 'If you can break this contract between us, then so can I. I'll go back to London and explain to the firm that I can't cope—and you can stay here to explain to Emily. OK?' Her determination and anger were a thin veneer over desperation, but she could only hope that he couldn't see that.

'Is this some new excuse to back out?' he sneered, but there was a thoughtful look on his face.

'Does it matter?' She was beginning to feel too tired to argue. 'Either I have a job or I don't. It's up to you.' It wasn't easy to defy him, but she couldn't let this go and keep her self-respect.

He was curiously still. 'Did you say you accepted responsibility for this mess?' he asked more quietly.

'Of course I do.' The taste of it was still sour in her mouth; she almost hoped he did decide to get rid of her. She felt as though she deserved it, anyway.

He looked broodingly at her for a long moment, then said, 'In that case I'll send that wretched student to you to confirm what I've told him. You can give him his cards—and find a replacement. All right?' He turned on his heel and left the room before she had a chance to reply.

She didn't know what to make of it. He evidently still blamed her, but he had somehow acknowledged her authority. Presumably she was still in charge. She looked down at her hands; they were shaking. She wished he'd sacked her. She didn't know what she wished. She wanted a shoulder to cry on—and the only shoulders broad enough had just walked out of the door.

Dinner was a nightmare. Emily had heard a garbled account of the incident, which Simon and she tried to minimise, while Pamela was inclined to make a major drama out of it. She was also avid for details, and quick to blame Holly.

'It might have been so dangerous.' She shuddered. 'I never liked that playground idea.'

'Children are always wandering off,' Emily said placidly. 'I could never keep track of Simon's antics when he was a boy, but he always turned up safe and well when he was hungry.' She smiled as though at a very private memory, and Holly thought she saw Simon's lips twitch in reluctant amusement. 'Anyway,' Emily's voice was practical, 'it was all a false alarm in the end, wasn't it?'

Holly met Simon's dark gaze. He nodded. 'Yes, it was,' he said decisively. 'A fuss about nothing, in fact. And I don't think it's likely to happen again.'

It was a totally unexpected assertion of confidence in

her. Holly was only too aware of how little she had done to deserve it and, for once, she could find nothing to say. The heightened colour on Pamela's cheekbones suggested that she, too, was surprised by Simon's declaration. She opened her mouth as if to object, but something in his face stopped her.

It was Emily who broke the long, awkward silence which followed. 'Do you realise it's only three weeks until the summer fête?' she asked cheerfully.

'What fête is that?' Holly asked politely, since neither of the others seemed to want to discuss it.

'It's the village fête,' Pamela was quick to inform her, in a tone which suggested that Holly should have known. 'It's held in the grounds of the Court every summer.'

Simon nodded. 'Second Saturday in July. It's an immovable feast, I'm afraid—we should have mentioned it to you earlier. We'll either have to shut the house to visitors that day, or find some way of combining the two.' He didn't sound at all enthusiastic about either option.

Emily began to look worried, but Pamela interrupted before Holly could speak. 'You can't possibly open that weekend, surely? The village comes first, after all.'

Simon's glance at her was slightly sardonic though his smile kept the worst of the edge from his voice. 'I don't remember your being that enthusiastic last year when Grandma tried to rope you in.' Not that he sounded particularly keen himself. Resigned, possibly. He turned to Holly. 'What do you think?'

Slightly surprised to be consulted, she tried to gather her thoughts. There didn't really seem to be a problem, and she said as much. 'As long as the fête committee don't mind, I should think the visitors will consider it an added attraction—and the village might find it raises more money than usual,' she added with a glance at Pamela. 'What date is it?' she asked Emily.

'July the tenth,' she said, and smiled at Simon. 'That will be nice, dear, won't it?'

His response could only, Holly thought, be called guarded. 'We'll see.'

She was intrigued and since, despite everything, he seemed to be on reasonable terms with her, she followed it up later that evening.

'What's the significance of July the tenth?' she asked.

He looked down at her, his expression a mixture of wry gloom and reluctant amusement. 'It's my birthday,' he admitted. 'Cancer, remember?'

Hesitantly, she touched his arm. 'Simon. . .' she began.

'Yes?' He looked at her, not drawing away, not responding.

'It's just that I wanted to say thank you.' The quick frown revealed his surprise. 'For giving me another chance this afternoon.' And for not saying anything in front of Pamela, but she could hardly say that.

His arm moved from under hers, his expression clearing to its familiar reserve. 'We were both to blame. Now it's up to you to make sure that nothing like that ever happens again,' he added, the steel clear in his voice.

Whatever she might have said to that clear warning was prevented by Pamela's reappearance. 'Am I interrupting a business conference?' she suggested archly.

'Not at all. Holly and I were just saying goodnight. Shall I run you home now?'

And that was that. Reprieve, not pardon, after all. Thoughtfully, Holly made her way to bed.

CHAPTER FIVE

SUMMER drew on faster than Holly could ever have expected. London seemed like another existence. She went back to the flat several times to check that all was well; she had called in at the office to report progress, and had received her boss's assent to her continued presence at the Court. But reality was here at the house, where visitors flocked every weekend and the people in the nearby town were beginning to treat her as a resident rather than a tourist. She had even been invited to the local primary school's end-of-term play as a 'thank you' for when she'd arranged a special guided tour of the house for the pupils doing a local history project.

As the second Saturday in July drew nearer, everything seemed to become progressively more chaotic.

'Don't worry, dear,' Emily said blithely when Holly sank her head in her hands. 'You don't have to do anything about the fête itself; in fact, I doubt whether the committee would let you.'

Nothing at all to do—except try to cope with the extra influx of visitors, find out whether there was any conflict between the needs of those who came to see the house and those who wanted only to visit the fête, and resolve the arguments which arose between the regular members of the staff and those taken on to cope with the extra numbers.

'London beginning to seem appealing again?' Simon suggested when she was briefly goaded into mentioning some of her problems, but he winced when she mentioned the fête. Later that day he went off in search of his grandmother, and Holly heard the sound of his raised voice. She wasn't surprised, however, when he emerged from the encounter with a look of defeat on his face.

'I usually try to avoid this particular festival,' he admitted.

'How often do you succeed?' Holly wondered.

'Oh, I can be very determined when I want to be,' he told her. She could believe it. Then he spoiled the effect by confessing with a wide grin. 'I manage to avoid about one in three. But I suspect I'm cornered this time.'

'What's so bad about it?' This year was going to be complicated by the tourists, but she could imagine that, in other circumstances, it might even be fun. Still, men didn't always see things in the same light.

Simon gave her a look which contained exasperation as well as private amusement. 'You'll see,' was all he would say.

The arrangements for the fête seemed to be well in hand. The committee of the WI bustled round organising cake-stalls, where Pamela had apparently agreed to preside, bric-a-brac, tombola, nearly new, and a variety of other entertainments including skittles and a 'test your strength' machine. It was all obviously a well-practised routine in which everything, including the site of each still, was governed by precedent. There was even, Holly discovered with amusement, a fortune-teller. She shouldn't have been surprised, she supposed. It was Emily's day, after all.

On the morning of the tenth, everything seemed to conspire to suggest that the day would be a success. Holly had wondered whether she should give Simon a birthday present; after all, she was only his employee. In the end, however, she hadn't been able to resist. She was treated as one of the family, by Emily at least, and it would be embarrassing to be the only one with nothing to offer to celebrate the day. That, at least, was how she justified her purchase to herself when she found the delicate little silver model of a seventeenth-century ship in an antique shop and thought how well it would fit in the library under one of the nautical paintings which were among his many interests.

When, at breakfast, he opened the small parcel, his wide smile of delight confirmed the rightness of her choice. He sat for a moment cradling the little ship.

'It's perfect,' he said, looking across the table at her, his dark eyes warm with genuine delight. 'Thank you.'

'Happy birthday,' she muttered awkwardly. Irrationally she felt her pulse quicken under his evident appreciation, however impersonal it might be. She found she couldn't meet his gaze, and looked down at her hands as they knotted the napkin on her lap. He was bending now to kiss Emily in affectionate thanks for her present, and it gave her a chance to recover slightly.

It didn't, however stop her starting the day feeling almost tipsy with happiness. Her new scarlet silk shirt was like a banner celebrating her mood. Outside, the sun was shining, the scent of new-mown grass filled the air, and fat bees bumbled among the heady riot of flowers. Every colour was a touch brighter than normal, each scent more intoxicating. The sun glinted on the lake, turning it to precious silver and the thick reeds round its bank to emerald.

She had half expected to meet Simon down by the water, and was a little disappointed to discover that he had not been seen there that morning. 'Busy up at the house, I expect,' she was told.

But Holly hadn't seen him there since breakfast. He was being very elusive today. Then she checked herself.

Was she really mooning round like a love-struck adolescent trying 'accidentally' to bump into the object of her fancy? Humiliated, she realised that that was exactly what she was doing. The only consolation was that it hadn't worked. She couldn't imagine what she'd say to Simon if she did manage to bump into him now. The colours of the day dimmed slightly for her, but a saving sense of humour at least allowed her to smile, however wryly, at her own folly before going off to see where her help was needed.

Nowhere, it seemed. Everyone appeared to have his or her own task well in hand, and Holly was left with little to do except stroll around. Emily firmly took fifty pence from her as an entry fee, and told her to go and enjoy the fête. 'Mind you visit everything,' she called after her.

If she didn't quite do everything, she did, rather to her own surprise, manage to enjoy herself. Looking around, she thought the fête could seldom have been busier; plenty of the tourists who had come to see the house were finding the stalls an unexpected and welcome addition to the day's entertainment. One large American family seemed particularly enchanted, and Holly wondered if they thought this sort of thing happened every week. Perhaps she should do some buying herself.

As she browsed among the discarded romances and thrillers on the second-hand bookstall she heard Simon's name mentioned by a large woman standing near by. She still hadn't caught sight of him, and the temptation to eavesdrop was irresistible. As she thumbed unseeing through a lurid-looking paperback, she listened to the earnest discussion. Which had nothing to do with old books.

'So, young Simon looks as though he's ready to settle

down at last, eh?' *Young* Simon? He was thirty-three—she had learned that this morning.

The other woman looked significantly over her shoulder towards the cake-stall. 'Yes. And I know someone apart from Emily who's going to be glad of it.'

Her companion followed her glance, and sniffed dismissively. 'She would. She's been hanging round in the wings for long enough.' A pause for thought was followed by a shrug. 'Still, I suppose it's a good enough match. Her family's been in the neighbourhood for ages, and it's about time Simon began to think about a family.' She looked around her. 'It's one thing, and a good thing too if you ask me, to open the Court to the public—it's given the old place a bit of life—but he can't want it to pass out of the family.'

No. Holly supposed that made some sort of sense. She replaced the book she'd been looking at and picked up another at random.

The other woman seemed to have more sympathy for Pamela. 'Well, the girl's been keen on him for long enough. She deserves some luck.'

The response was cynical. 'Perhaps. Rumour has it that Captain Weston's having to sell off more land.' The meaningful glance lingered again on the tall, blonde girl. 'It would certainly suit her if Simon really had made up his mind to settle.'

A sense of distaste overcame Holly. Without really looking at what she was buying, she handed over some coins for the book she held and turned away. Eavesdropping never did anyone any good; it had only confirmed what she had already known, anyway. It *was* a very suitable match. And if Pamela *was* as interested in Simon's money as in himself, what did that matter? Simon certainly didn't give the impression of being a man passionately in love.

She walked slowly away from the noisy crowd. A glance down at the book in her hand told her that she'd acquired a very battered copy of a novel that she'd already read and disliked. With a humourless smile, she dropped it in the first litter-bin she passed. The day, which had started so well, had lost much of its sparkle. As she found herself alone by the lakeside she began to wonder just why she had been so repelled by the conversation she had heard.

The feelings which Simon stirred in her were uncomfortable and disturbing and had brought her nothing like the bubbling ecstasy which Jenny always seemed to feel, but they had awakened something which she had not known she possessed. She didn't know exactly when it had happened, but she knew with a fierce certainty that the thought of Simon as a partner in such a cold-blooded arrangement appalled her. He had a temper; surely he had other passions too? They couldn't all have been buried with Laura. And if they had been, it would almost be better for him not to marry at all. Did a family name, however old, really matter so much against the hypocrisy of such a soulless relationship?

She shook her head. It was time to go back and mingle with the visitors. That was her job, after all.

Unfortunately, the cake-stall had been the first to sell all its produce, and that meant that Pamela, too, was mingling. Holly saw her and would have found business elsewhere, but wasn't given the chance.

'Holly!' The clear voice halted her. 'I hope you're enjoying the fête?' The smile and apparent friendliness were unexpected but, on the whole, a relief.

'Very much,' she agreed. 'So are the visitors.'

A flicker of distaste marred Pamela's expression. 'Yes. I'm sure they are,' she agreed neutrally. 'Of course,' she added more firmly, walking Holly to a less busy part of the lawn, 'they should count themselves lucky to be here.'

Holly raised an eyebrow. Danfield Court was a delightful house, but it wasn't Buckingham Palace. Pamela saw the expression and smiled.

'I only meant that the Court won't be open again next year.' The flat statement contrasted with the poised smile, which didn't alter. Nor did it touch the blue eyes.

Holly felt something twist inside her. 'What do you mean? Simon's said nothing about it to me,' she protested sharply.

'There's no reason why he should, is there?' Her tone was all sweet reason, the underlying satisfaction obvious.

Of course not. She wouldn't even be here then. Part of her job was to train a local manager to take over from her. Somehow, the illusion that this summer would last forever had crept up on her, defeating all her common sense just when she was congratulating herself on behaving sensibly.

'No, I suppose not,' she admitted reluctantly. 'But I still don't see——'

'It won't be appropriate, not once we're married,' Pamela told her.

It was the first time that anyone had suggested to Holly that there was something improper about opening a house to the public, but Pamela sounded adamant.

Holly tried to sound neutral. 'Emily will be disappointed,' she commented.

Irritation showed briefly on the other woman's immaculate face. 'I'm sure she'll understand. Once Simon and I are married——' the repetition seemed almost deliberate, as though Pamela wanted to probe for something she suspected but could not prove

'—there will be quite a few changes. Naturally there will always be a place for Emily at the Court.'

Naturally. Holly's blood ran cold at the chilling prospect conjured up by Pamela's words. If she said anything now, it would probably be unforgivable, but there seemed no immediately convenient reason to break off this conversation. Pamela, it was clear, had not quite finished.

'I hear you gave Simon a present this morning?' she asked.

'Yes,' Holly confirmed, unwilling to say more. Somewhere she felt a faint glow of pleasure that Simon had mentioned her gift.

Elegantly plucked brow lifted. 'A little unusual, wouldn't you say? You aren't one of the family, after all, are you?'

Politeness, even caution, had its limits. 'No, I'm not,' Holly agreed. 'But then, neither are you, yet. Are you?' she added with a tight-lipped smile. 'Excuse me.' She turned and walked quickly away before Pamela could find an appropriate response.

She had to get away. On duty or not, she did not want to be anywhere where that woman could find her, or she wouldn't answer for her actions. The house was no sanctuary. Not even her office would be secure from interruptions.

She almost blundered into the red and white striped tent before she saw it. The fortune-teller. Of course. No one would look for her there, and five minutes of outrageous nonsense just might restore her sense of proportion. Brushing the canvas flap aside, she slipped into the tent's dim interior to confront the bizarrely clad figure bent over a small table.

'And I thought you were the one person I could rely on *not* to have any part in this idiocy!' growled a familiar voice in tones of extreme exasperation.

She sat down abruptly and looked at the 'gypsy' opposite her. There was no mistaking those dark brown eyes and strong features beneath the gaudy turban. The absurd contrast with her recent encounter was too much for her. A bubble of laughter started somewhere inside, erupting into a convulsion of mirth which she couldn't control. Simon watched her, maintaining his own air of injured gloom for a long moment before giving in and letting his warm laughter mingle with hers.

'How on earth did Emily con you into this?' Holly demanded when at last she sobered enough to speak.

'How does she con anyone into anything? You know her almost as well as I do—how could I have got out of it?'

'You do this *every* year?' No wonder he'd kept quiet about it, although she had a sneaking suspicion he was enjoying himself.

'Whenever I haven't managed to find a pressing previous engagement,' he admitted. 'And why are *you* here?'

It wasn't a question she intended to answer. He shrugged and then smiled, leaving her slightly breathless, as though inviting her to join the conspiracy. He reached out an arm to the assortment of props beside him, and picked up a deck of cards. 'Right, since you *are* here, I suppose I'd better earn my keep and see if I can discover what the fates have in store for you. Take a card.'

Holly hadn't expected that. It was oddly disturbing, but there was a challenge in his eyes which she couldn't ignore. She reached out and took a card. Queen of Hearts.

He accepted it back without comment and then dealt out more cards in some sort of pattern. Gibberish, she thought. But he was evidently practised at it. He studied the layout; her queen with a king next to it and a confusion of other court cards around it.

'Well?' she asked cheerfully. 'Tell me the worst.'

'No worst at all,' he rejected indignantly. 'Love, wealth, happiness and a long life. Of course. All to be found in the arms of a dark-haired lover,' he added glibly, picking up the cards and stacking them neatly to one side. She watched with suspicion. She had no need to use much imagination to recall the dark hair concealed beneath that ridiculous turban. He looked up, his smile deriding his own patter. 'How did I do?'

'Terrible,' she told him bluntly. 'It's probably a good thing your clients have to pay in advance.'

He looked pained, then suspicious. 'That's a point. Did *you* pay?'

She grinned. 'No, and I don't intend to.'

His attempt to look insulted didn't really work. 'Cheated again.' Then, looking at her more seriously, he asked, 'Why on earth *did* you come in here? You bolted through that tent-flap like a ferret down a rabbit-hole,' he remembered.

'Thanks.' After that unpleasant encounter with Pamela she hadn't had much dignity left. It seemed a long time ago. Somehow this tent was isolated from the rest of the world, somewhere where she could laugh over nonsense and temporarily set aside the emotional confusion which was rapidly overwhelming her. 'I was looking for a bolt-hole,' she admitted.

He straightened, reaching up to tug the gaudy turban from his head and run his hands through the unruly dark mass of his hair. 'Yes? Who was hunting you?' he asked almost gently.

She shrugged. In the circumstances it wasn't a question she felt like answering. 'No one, really. It just got a bit hectic for a while out there.' She stood up. 'I'd better go and leave you to your paying customers.'

He stood with her, shrugging off the heavy robe that covered his more familiar dark corduroy trousers and cotton shirt. 'Gypsy Rose has earned a break. Will you join me?'

She was mad. She had to be. Why else would she emerge from the tent into the bright sunlight with Simon beside her, knowing that there was every chance Pamela would be waiting? There was something exhilarating about it, and she was almost disappointed to discover no sign of the other woman as they strolled across the lawn.

Simon drew a deep breath, as though celebrating his release from the cramped and stuffy tent. 'That's better.' He glanced sideways at Holly. 'I need to stretch my legs. Fancy a walk?'

She looked around. Everyone seemed busy and cheerful, no one seemed to need her. 'I really ought——' she began, but wasn't sorry to be overruled.

'Even you can take a break. Or don't you trust your own organisation?' he asked provocatively, and there was only one possible reply to that.

'Of course I do.' She fell into step beside him. What did it matter, after all, who saw them together?

They didn't speak much till they reached the belvedere. No one else was there, and they could look down on the busy scenes below and the peaceful woodland in the distance. Simon leaned against the balustrade with a sigh of satisfaction.

'That's better.'

She felt herself begin to relax. It was too good a day to let Pamela's snobbery, or thoughts of the future, upset her. 'Yes,' she agreed.

He turned lazily, so that his back was to the view, and faced her. 'So why did you need a bolt-hole?' he asked quietly.

Startled, Holly didn't know what to say. 'Nothing. No reason,' she denied incoherently.

'No reason?' He didn't even begin to believe her, and she knew it.

His sombre gaze was still regarding her steadily, demanding an answer.

'Let's just say that it's private,' she managed. It might be rude, but surely he would leave it at that?

Apparently not. There was something remorseless about his determination, and Holly wished they were back among the crowds where she could find some excuse to slip away. Up here, high above all the visitors, there was nowhere to run to.

'I don't like anyone upsetting my guests,' he told her.

Her laugh was brittle. She'd spent a large part of today reminding herself of the nature of their relationship. *Guest* had nothing to do with it.

'That hardly describes me,' she pointed out. 'I work for you.'

'All the more reason to know what's wrong,' he said imperturbably. 'Come on, Holly, I know it's not some crisis with your work this time; you wouldn't hide that.'

She wished he were wrong.

'Just leave it,' she snapped. 'I can deal with it myself. I thought we came up here to relax?'

'Your mistake,' he told her, watching her closely. Then he seemed to reach a decision. 'All right, I'll leave it for the moment. Let's admire the view.'

Any reprieve was better than none. She looked obediently over the river and lake, feeling the quick smart of tears behind her eyes. 'I'm going to miss all this,' she said quietly.

'What do you mean?' He sounded startled.

She looked across at him. 'Next year, when I'm not

here,' she reminded him. 'I'll be going in October. Remember?'

'Of course. I'd almost forgotten,' he admitted. 'You'll always be welcome back, though. You know that.'

She knew precisely the opposite.

'Anyway,' he pointed out, 'I can't imagine Grandma letting you slip off just like that.'

Pamela had not shown any sign of giving Emily any say in the matter at all. 'No, of course not.' Holly tried to sound positive, but even she could hear the hint of melancholy in her voice. Simon looked as though he was about to start asking questions again, and she had no intention of answering them. When she spoke again she was deliberately brisk. 'Anyone would think I'm off tomorrow. There's three months until the season ends—and you, at least, will want to celebrate that, surely?'

He chuckled. 'I suppose you're right. You'd think me mad if I didn't. But I have to admit that the opening has brought the Court back to life. I'd almost forgotten what it could be like,' he added, almost to himself.

She was amazed. 'You're not saying you *don't* think it was such a crazy idea after all?'

'Let's just say that it's not been the disaster I expected,' he conceded. Holly felt her throat thicken with sudden emotion.

'I couldn't have done it without your help, however reluctant,' she told him.

He grinned, dispelling the serious moment. 'You'll have to slip in incognito next year, and make sure that it's still being run to your standards,' he joked.

Holly wasn't joking. She was stunned. 'But I thought——'

'What?' The quick frown creased his heavy brows.

'I thought you weren't opening again next season,' she explained simply.

It was his turn to look startled. 'What do you mean?'

'What I said,' she insisted. 'Pamela told me——'

'Pamela told you we weren't opening next year?' he asked. 'Why were you discussing it with her?' Much of the friendliness had gone from his attitude, but she wouldn't let him intimidate her.

'I wasn't the one doing the discussing,' she recalled, her tone dry.

'When was this?' he demanded.

'About an hour ago,' she admitted carelessly.

No one could call Simon a fool. He was still for a moment. 'I see. And what else did she say?'

The ground under Holly's feet might have been made of heavy stone slabs, but suddenly it seemed unstable. 'Nothing. I don't remember. We were just chatting.'

'Just chatting. And then you bolted into my tent as though in desperate need of sanctuary,' he reminded her. 'Tell me about it. What else did you chat about—apart from next year's plans for the Court?' The thread of suspicion in his voice was twisting into something much stronger but Holly, too, was angry. It was bad enough being insulted by Pamela; she was not going to be Simon's victim, too.

'What do you think?' she snapped, for once not guarding her tongue. 'We discussed you, of course!'

He relaxed, or at least he seemed to. He leaned back against the wall. 'Did you, indeed?'

The brief spurt of rage had gone. Holly shook her head wearily. 'No. I'd already been warned off you weeks ago,' she told him, and turned away. She might as well go back to the house. There was bound to be something she could busy herself with there.

Hard hands on her shoulders swung her back to him. '*Who* warned you? Pamela?'

She tried to wrench free and failed, so she stood still under his grasp, hoping he could not feel the rapid pulse of her blood beneath his fingers. 'Who else?' she asked as coldly as she could. 'Or have you a whole harem laying claim to you?'

It might have been more sensible not to provoke him, but she was beyond being sensible. When his fingers flexed hard in her shoulders she thought he was going to shake her. But he didn't.

'*No one*,' he said, his voice taut with anger, 'has any claim on me.' For a moment he seemed about to fling her away from him, then his grip changed and suddenly she was held tightly against the wall of his chest.

'Perhaps *this* will convince you.' His head came down and his mouth slanted savagely across hers.

It was a hard kiss, bruising in its intensity, and when she moaned a protest his grip only tightened. She struggled, but it was no use. She was fighting herself as well as him. She could only submit to the fierce embrace.

She couldn't tell exactly when it changed, when demand became persuasion and his lips began to move coaxingly against hers. Her lips parted, and when his arms relaxed their iron hold her own stole up to hold his powerful shoulder, accepting the support she had always known they could give. His hands moved against her back, drawing her closer into his hips while his mouth plundered hers with devastating sweetness.

And then it was over. He let her go and stepped back from her so suddenly that she had to grasp the stone ballustrade for support. Its rough edge dug into her soft palm; reality intruding on a sweet dream. She stared at him, her grey eyes blurred with dawning passion.

His face was grim. '*That* should answer your question,' he told her in a savage undertone, and strode away from her before she could even lift a hand to her bruised mouth.

What question? Something about people having a claim on him, she vaguely remembered. If that had been an answer, it wasn't one she understood.

Slowly, as though not quite able to trust her legs, she sat down on the low wall. What had happened? What had she done to drive him to that furious kiss which had seemed both insult and rapture? It made no sense at all. Earlier that day, hadn't she been wondering if Simon had any passion left in him? Her smile twisted in ironic mockery. Well, at least that question was answered now. And if she'd ever wondered about herself, she realised with a kind of despair, she had her answer to that, too. She wasn't sure how she was ever going to be able to face Simon again.

Afterwards she had no idea how long she'd spent sitting up there, letting her thought drift, and allowing herself to store up memories of something that might have arisen from anger but which had somehow been both primitive and glorious.

Eventually the shadows lengthened, and she began to make her way back along the beech walk and out on to the lawns. Most of the visitors had gone, and the women were busy packing up the trestle-tables.

One of them greeted her with a beaming smile. 'Best day we've ever had for the fête, I reckon,' she said, indicating two heavy bags of coins. 'It was a good day for the Court when you came to open it up. Like a breath of fresh air, it's been.'

The unreserved approval made Holly smile. At least someone thought she was doing the right thing. 'Thanks, Mrs Morris,' she managed. 'I'm glad the day's been a success.'

Over the woman's shoulder she glimpsed Pamela walking quickly over the grass in their direction.

Pamela saw her at the same moment and stopped abruptly. She stared at Holly for a long, hard moment and then, deliberately, turned her back and walked away.

Holly supposed she must have said whatever was polite to Mrs Morris, but she had no idea what. Pamela's expression had told her far more than she wanted to know. She looked from the lawn up towards the belvedere which was just visible high on the hillside. Two figures standing up there, particularly when one was, like her, wearing red, would be quite visible to anyone below who was interested. Most people would hardly have spared them more than a moment's glance. But Pamela, Holly realised, had been watching for considerably longer than that.

CHAPTER SIX

THAT night, troubled thoughts and half understood, newly awakened feelings kept Holly awake. She wasn't quite sure how she had got through the rest of that afternoon. Pamela had, fortunately, not put in another appearance, but Emily's cheerful enthusiasm and eagerness to discuss the day's success had been almost as hard to bear as the way Simon had left the room only minutes after she had entered. Oh, he'd said something polite, and spoken of making an important call, but it had been clear he had no wish for her company. His absence might have saved her some embarrassment—she still had no idea just how she was going to work with him again—but that abrupt departure had hurt.

Luckily, she hadn't had to face him at dinner. Emily had insisted on a birthday celebration in town and had eventually, and reluctantly, accepted Holly's insistence that it really would be inappropriate for her to join the small group of family and friends. As she lay restlessly in bed, having rejected the thought of any food for herself, Holly realised that Pamela would almost certainly be there. Would she refer to the incident she had seen? Probably not. She would blame it on Holly and merely try even harder to make Simon commit himself. What about Simon? It wouldn't trouble him much either, Holly reluctantly concluded. He couldn't know that something done in a moment of anger could have affected her so profoundly.

She still couldn't work out how it had happened, or why. She could understand his anger at learning that he had been discussed by Pamela and herself, but that didn't account for the kiss. Could he have known where Pamela was, and made a deliberate attempt to annoy her? Or had it been some unaccountable male response which she might have understood better had she been more experienced? Probably. The limitations of her own experience had certainly been brought home to her. Nothing in her own life, or in Jenny's frequent accounts of her infatuations, had prepared her for that shattering kiss. Or the utter humiliation of knowing that what for him had been only an outlet for annoyance could so unbalance the very foundations of her life.

For years now she had *known*, not just believed, that she 'wasn't the type' who fell in love. She had looked forward to one day being an aunt to her sister's children while she continued with her own successful career. In one dizzying moment she had discovered just how little she actually cared about her career—that all her busy ambitions had been the cover for an aching need to have her own home and family. Simon's family. It wasn't what anyone would call a modern attitude, and she had never thought she would come to understand it, never mind share it. She turned restlessly in bed, trying to recover a fast-vanishing sense of humour. She needed to laugh at herself and her absurd dreams, otherwise she wasn't sure if she would be able to stop crying.

Sleep proved elusive and in the end she gave up and took an early-morning shower. It was quite light, but nothing was astir. She dressed, then slipped quietly down the broad staircase and out on to the terrace. A few birds twittered sleepily, but nothing else disturbed the peace. At least here, unlike in London, she could walk alone in the early hours without fearing muggers or choking in the smothering fumes of traffic. She grimaced. In London she had never passed a sleepless night which had driven her out into the dawn to seek comfort.

She must have walked for about an hour before she realised she would have to go back to the house if she wanted no one to notice her return or comment on her unusually early activity. At least she felt soothed as she turned back, even if she knew that she had resolved nothing.

She wasn't looking where she was going as she walked up the old steps to the glass doors. Nor was the man who was just coming out through them. They collided with some force, and he automatically reached out to steady her before letting his hands drop quickly from her as though, she thought, he couldn't bear to prolong the contact.

'Sorry,' she muttered, taking a step backwards.

'My fault.' Somehow, conventional politeness was a lifebelt in a sea of potential embarrassment. Then she realised he was wearing his dark suit and carrying an attaché case.

'You're going away?' she asked involuntarily, before she remembered that she had no right to.

'Yes.' His response was curt. 'I've some urgent business to see to.'

On a Sunday? But it was quite clear that she was in his way, holding him up. Holly stepped carefully aside so that there was no longer the slightest danger that he might brush against her as he passed. Something flickered in the dark eyes as he noted her movement, and his mouth tightened.

'Have a good journey.' It didn't sound nearly as cheerful and detached as she'd intended, but perhaps he wouldn't notice the slightly breathless catch in her throat.

Evidently not. 'Thanks.' He took another step

towards the door as though he could not wait to get away, and then he hesitated, turning back. Only a couple of feet separated them. How was it possible to feel how unbridgeable that gap was at the same time as remembering so vividly just how wide those shoulders had felt under her hands?

He was frowning steadily and his voice was harsh when he spoke. 'I have to leave.' He might have been trying to convince himself as much as her. 'We'll talk when I get back.'

Instinctively, Holly shook her head. She wasn't going to court danger. 'There's nothing to talk about,' she insisted.

For a moment she thought he was going to step across that gap and touch her, but he glanced at his watch instead and swore beneath his breath before glaring at her again. 'There's plenty to discuss and you know it,' he contradicted, turning and stepping out through the french windows before she could repeat her automatic denial.

She clutched the collar of her blouse tightly against her throat as she watched him walk away. Almost as though she were cold. But it was an internal chill which not even the bright heat of a July morning could dispel. She couldn't quite believe that his sudden departure had nothing to do with yesterday. He might even want to face her as little as she felt she could cope with him. Was the 'talk' he promised—or threatened—going to mean her replacement on the job? Oh, he wouldn't do anything to harm her position with the firm, but perhaps he might feel it was inconvenient to have her around any longer. Or perhaps Pamela had put her foot down last night?

It wasn't easy to seem her normal self in front of Emily. In fact, she wasn't sure she'd succeeded. Once or twice she had felt the elderly lady's faded eyes dwelling thoughtfully on her, and had braced herself for questions which never came. She was grateful for that silence, and that there were still the demands of the public to keep her occupied. Now that the school holidays were under way, they were busier than ever with large numbers of families making the most of an unexpectedly fine summer.

Simon didn't come home that week, or the next. Emily spoke to him several times on the phone, but there had been no messages for Holly. She thought she was glad of that, but could not quite dispel the uncharacteristic depression which tended to steal up on her whenever she had time for reflection. Somehow, all her habitual optimism had drained away and even her work, which had once given her such a sense of achievement, had begun to seem almost mechanical.

By now, of course, the routine of running the house over the weekends was well established. Although Holly had a constant stream of minor decisions to make, she was confident that she had set up a system which would run well under the local manager she was beginning to train. If Simon really did mean to re-open the Court next year, he should have no problems.

In his continued absence her own problems remained in a sort of limbo. Even Pamela was studiously polite to her on the few occasions that they met. Luckily Simon's absence seemed to mean that the other woman saw no need to put in more than the occasional token visit to the Court. Not that Holly made the mistake of taking Pamela's civility for forgiveness; the hostility was still there.

August began with a message from Simon to expect him on the following Sunday, and suddenly Pamela was everywhere again. She seemed to have developed a keen and unlikely interest in the running of the open days; had Simon made it clear that they would continue?

Reluctantly, Holly answered the other woman's questions. She did not want to, but her professionalism made her explain what she could, except on subjects which she considered private to her employer. When she referred Pamela to Simon over some question of finance, however, the tall woman just shrugged her elegant shoulders.

'Of course he'll tell me,' she said with impatient contempt, and Holly wondered whether Simon would let her know that he thought her discretion misplaced.

Over the summer a few staff had left and replacements been found. The new playground attendant was an enthusiast who had just qualified as a PE teacher and was waiting to take up his new job; after watching him covertly for some time, Holly was deeply relieved to realise that he was completely reliable. The river-trips, too, were going well. In fact they were so successful that the man who was running them asked if he could have an assistant so that they could reduce the risks to the crowds around the landing-stage.

For once, Holly wanted to talk to Simon. The trips around the lake had become *his* project, and he had personally chosen the staff involved. Now they needed someone in a hurry, and he seemed to be out of contact. She tried his office, but was told he was 'unavailable'.

In the end she had to trust her own judgement, even though it had been shaken by the incident in the playground. She appointed a young man who seemed to be well qualified, if a bit inexperienced. She thought he would be all right, though, under her own close supervision and that of the regular boatman. After all, hadn't she had her own recent problems with accusations of youth and inexperience?

The day that Simon was due back was even busier than usual. Pamela was around, playing the gracious hostess, Holly decided as she watched her pause to talk to the more sedate or well-dressed visitors. She couldn't help noticing how the tall blonde drifted away from contact with noisy family parties. Still, she supposed she should be grateful that the other woman had decided, for whatever reasons, to support the open days. She even offered to go and check that all was well down at the river. Since Holly had at that moment been dealing with two problems and a telephone call simultaneously she had accepted the offer gratefully. She could always make her own checks later.

It was almost four o'clock before she found the time. As she walked quickly out of the house she couldn't help wondering with wry honesty how much her eagerness to make her escape had to do with a desire not to be alone in her office when Simon returned. More than a little, she suspected, and increased her pace across the lawn.

There was a little more noise than usual coming from the area of the boathouse, and Holly thought she heard some cheerful shouts of encouragement. About what? She had to squeeze her way through the crowd of young people to find out. There was a notice on the big river launch apologising for the temporary suspension of trips round the lake, 'owing to mechanical problems,' and offering children rides in the sailing dinghy instead. There was no sign at all of the senior boatman.

The queue was calling out good-natured encouragement to the two figures in the little red-sailed dinghy. Holly couldn't see very clearly, but it looked as though the child was trying to steer while being instructed by the new assistant. Not much progress was being made. Nor, she realised with growing horror, was either of them wearing a life-jacket.

She strode over to the new notice and removed it, explaining as soothingly as she could to the now impatient crowd that the dinghy rides were cancelled. Her fixed smile began to make her jaw ache. As she tried to calm protests and return money, she kept stealing glances towards the lake. The boat wasn't going anywhere in particular, and she thanked heaven that there was very little wind. She wished frantically that she knew something, anything, about boats. Then she could take the small motor launch out to tow them back in.

'Shouldn't they be coming back? They've had their half-hour,' grumbled a disappointed lad of about fourteen.

'They'll be back in a few minutes,' she replied automatically, hoping she was right. She also hoped fervently that the parents of the child in the boat weren't near, or beginning to realise what was happening. She wanted to clear this up *before* anyone thought about the risks. Then she remembered the new playground attendant. He might know about boats.

Taking a last, urgent look out over the water, and crossing her fingers that the deceptively pretty tableau of the little boat with its red sails flapping placidly over the calm water would not change into something more sinister as soon as she turned her back, Holly began to make her way away from the lake, fighting the temptation to run.

She was conscious of a desperate need for haste, glancing back from time to time to confirm that all was still well, when she cannoned into a broad chest. Hard hands held her off. Simon's face was almost white and his eyes burned with a fury she had never faced before.

'Where the *hell* do you think you're going?' he demanded, his lips thinned to a pale line.

'To fetch someone. The lake——' she began incoherently. But she didn't need to explain. Someone had clearly already told him.

He let go of her shoulders as he looked beyond her to the water. She thought she heard him swear and, if anything, his expression grew grimmer. Dismissing her without another word, he broke into a run, heading for the launch. She turned. In the few seconds she had been away, something disastrous must have happened to the inexperienced pair in the dinghy.

Its red sails no longer fluttered jauntily, instead they lay flat against the water surface while two figures could be seen clinging to the boat's upturned hull. Their cries for help echoed over the water.

She was running before she had fully realised what had happened, but Simon's long legs had taken him to the motor-boat minutes before she arrived, panting, at the shore.

There was nothing she could do. She could only stand staring with the rest of the crowd as they watched Simon in the launch as it neared the capsized boat. Most of them, she realised, were enjoying the drama. It might almost have been a spectacle laid on for their entertainment, she thought with sudden, fear-bred anger. She tried to tune out their comments, focusing with desperate intensity on what was happening on the water, dimly conscious that her anguished concern was for Simon and what this must be doing to him as well as for the two people struggling in the water.

Afterwards she realised that the incident had lasted only a few minutes from the time the launch's engine had roared into life under Simon's control. At the time it seemed like hours before he hauled first the child, then the younger attendant, dripping, into the boat and turned back to the shore. When Holly went to meet them, offering an eager hand to the excited but soaked child, he brushed her aside.

'I'll deal with this. Send the nurse from the playground to me here. I'll see *you* later, back at the house.' He turned back to the two he had rescued, dismissing her before she could utter a word. Behind her, willing hands were reaching out to offer help and congratulations. She wasn't needed. She could only do what he had asked—no, ordered—and wait for the full weight of his anger to fall.

It was a long wait. She tried to carry on the office work as though everything was normal, but she did not even begin to fool herself. The scene on the lake insisted on repeating itself, like an endless loop, in her brain. She couldn't begin to understand how it had happened. The older boatman had clearly not been present, but that did not explain why it hadn't been reported to her. It was one of her basic standing rules that she should know at once if anyone, for any reason, was absent. It was a rule designed both to keep things running smoothly when they were short-handed, and as a safety-net in case anyone thought they could manage more than was really possible. Which was what must have happened on the lake.

If Simon hadn't already dismissed the new boatman for endangering lives, it looked as though that would have to be her first job. And it was going to cause her far less heart-searching than she had felt when she had talked to the careless playground attendant.

Inevitably, her thoughts returned to Simon. She didn't think so much about what he was going to say to her as about what he must have felt when he'd realised what had happened. It must have seemed as though Laura's ghost was haunting him, as though the lake was inevitably going to produce tragedy. Thank heaven that he had turned up when he did; at least, this time, tragedy have been averted.

Her office door slammed open. Simon didn't even give her a chance to speak as he strode over to the desk.

'I want you out of this house tomorrow. Understand?' His voice was low, hard and furious. The hands resting on the desk in front of her were white-knuckled, as though physical violence was only being held at bay by an immense effort.

Stunned, both by his tone and by what he had said, Holly stared blindly back at him. Somewhere, a great wave of desolation was about to break, but bewilderment and dawning terror held it back.

'The child. . .? The boy. . .?' she stammered. 'Is he——' He had seemed fine as Simon had lifted him ashore, but had there been damage she hadn't known about?

He shook his head impatiently. 'He's OK. They both are. But that doesn't excuse what you've done. How *could* you?' he burst out with a kind of anguished fury. 'I thought at least I could trust you not to take any risks at the lake.'

'But I didn't!' she protested. 'I didn't know!' How weak that sounded—she *should* have known.

A look of something like disgust replaced the heat of rage and he straightened, looking down at her with contempt. Absently she noticed the oil-stains on his shirt-cuffs and the marks on his jacket where the lake water had dried.

'Don't lie to me. At least you ought to have the guts to face up to your responsibilities.'

As he had had to. Just how much responsibility did he feel for today?

'I'm not lying,' she insisted. It wouldn't do any good to cry, and she fought back the ridiculous swell of tears—and the absurd urge to reach out to him, to touch the passionate man she had so fleetingly known behind this chilling autocrat.

His shoulders seemed almost to sag as he thrust his hands in his pockets and continued to regard her as if he had never really seen her before. And as if she had just disappointed one last, vain hope.

'I've spoken to Dave,' he said, a frosty calm in his voice as he named the attendant. 'He admits he should never have tried to take the dinghy out; but *you* should have been able to prevent him.'

Holly was almost tired of defending herself against something she didn't understand. She had been prepared for his anger, expecting it, but what he was saying made no sense.

'I don't know what you're talking about,' she insisted. 'Of course I'd have stopped him if I'd known what he planned. But I didn't even know the senior boatman wasn't in today.'

Disbelief and distaste showed in his face. 'Dave phoned the house. He has witnesses to prove it—who will swear that they heard a woman answer to *your* name and tell him he could go ahead.'

'But that's impossible! I——'

'Either he and several other people are lying, or you are. This time, I think the majority wins.' He too sounded weary, anxious only to dispose of something peculiarly unpleasant. Then, as if goaded, he exploded, 'For heaven's sake, Holly, *why* did you do it? And why lie about it? I thought at least you had some integrity, even if you obviously can't cope with a job like this.'

The injustice of that stung. She pushed her chair sharply back and stood up. 'I'm *not* lying.' He was about to interrupt but she stopped him, shaking her head. 'No, I *don't* know how to account for what Dave said. All I know is that I haven't spoken to him all day.

In fact, *that* was the crime I was expecting you to accuse me of, not this——' she gestured helplessly '—this *rubbish*!'

She wasn't getting through to him at all. His set expression told her that he had made his decision, and had only scorn for what must seem like the feeblest of excuses.

'I said I would break your contract if I had to. I will. You can stay here tonight, but I don't want to see you after tomorrow morning.'

As simple as that. But he couldn't just move people round like counters even if he did have the authority, perhaps even the right, to sack her.

'What about your grandmother?' she asked quietly.

'If you value her peace of mind, you'll tell her that your firm has called you back to take on some new work. You can even say you'll keep in touch by phone. But I don't want to see you here.'

'Don't worry. You won't.' Anger at his condemnation of her, whatever his reasons, was beginning to overcome Holly's feelings of guilt. 'Are you going to tell my boss why I'm sacked, or shall I?' The defiant indifference was hollow as she fought off the recognition that her career was in ruins, but it helped her to face him.

He looked her over for a long minute before he shrugged. 'Neither. You're not sacked.' For a moment, joy and relief must have shown in her face because he crushed them easily with his next words. 'I just don't want you here. You can stay at home or go and see your family, for all I care. I'll go on paying your wages. Look on it as payment for the good work you did manage to do before you wrecked it all. I'll even send you the administrative paperwork to deal with if your *conscience*——' the stress made the word an ironic sneer '—insists that you earn your keep.'

The casual, almost patronising generosity, the reprieve which was only an insult, made her want to hit him and throw his offer back in his face. Only the knowledge that now she had nothing left but her career, not even the crumbled ruins of a romantic fantasy, made her grit her teeth and mutter, 'Thank you.' Then she remembered. 'But who'll run the estate? The new manager——'

'Isn't up to it yet. I know,' he interrupted ruthlessly. 'But that's not your concern any more, is it?' he pointed out. She didn't think he was going to say anything else, then he added, as though he couldn't quite help it, 'I'll be here. That's why I've been away so much lately; I've been settling with the London firm and selling out my share in it. I won't need a manager.'

Of course not. He had it all worked out. Defeat, and the need for private thought, drained what defiance she had left. 'Excuse me. I have to pack,' she muttered, and walked to the door.

She was almost there when he said, 'Holly?' in a quiet, altered, voice.

Reluctantly, drawn despite herself, she turned. 'Yes?' She stared at him, her eyes wide and bright with unshed tears, indulging in the luxury of a last long look at his dark Cavalier looks and powerful frame. Her eyes blurred and she didn't see the momentary softening of his expression before frustrated anger tightened his frown again.

'Nothing,' he said abruptly, adding as he turned away from her, 'I'm sure I can persuade Grandma to understand if you don't feel like joining us for dinner.'

She shut the door behind her, because she had the feeling that the heavy oak door would splinter if she let it slam with the full force of the urge that that order masked in hypocritcal concern left in her.

Later she was relieved not to have to face anyone.

She had packed her few clothes with even more care than usual, meticulously folding each item as though every crease mattered, but there was a limit to how long she could find tasks which would stave off her thoughts.

In a numb sort of way she wasn't surprised to be leaving. She felt she deserved something of the sort after today's catastrophe, even if she hadn't really believed it would happen. What made no sense at all were the accusations Simon had thrown at her. She *knew*, despite the fact that the day had been hectically busy, she couldn't possibly have forgotten if Dave had phoned her. In other circumstances she might have thought it was he who was lying in a desperate effort to save his job. But Simon had said he had witnesses. Other people had actually *heard* the conversation. And, anyway, Dave had never struck her as dishonest. A little young, possibly, but not a liar. So what did that make her? Simon had made it unpleasantly clear what he thought, but how on earth had such a disastrous confusion occurred?

Desperately, she thought back over the day, trying to remember who had been in the house. Emily, of course, but, even if that had not been too ridiculous a possibility to be worth considering, she had been busy showing visitors around. The housekeeper? But she would have passed any calls directly to Holly, or to someone in the family.

The family. That meant Simon or Emily, but there was one other person who treated the house as her own. When Pamela had come into the office to say she would go down to the river, had she really been a little more cheerful than usual? Had she, in fact, been anticipating trouble because she'd just taken a phone call intended for Holly? Impossible. She was being melodramatic.

Or was she? Holly remembered the look of enmity she had received on the day of the fête. Perhaps Pamela *would* do something to get her into trouble. She knew about the earlier incident, after all. Holly could even remember her arriving just as Simon had warned her against future disasters. She would know that he would not tolerate any more trouble, particularly if it was connected with the lake.

Holly didn't want to believe it. Could anyone really be that vindictive and callous? She would have had to have been indifferent not only to the hurt Simon would have had to suffer had he not arrived in time, but also to the lives of the people she had risked so carelessly. Even in a moment of blind rage it seemed unbelievable, but Holly could think of no other even remotely possible explanation of what had happened. And, she realised, there was no way at all of proving it. Pamela would deny it, of course. She might even be innocent, after all, and Simon's disgust would only deepen. Holly didn't think she could bear to imagine his expression if he knew what she was thinking. And what about Emily? Any such unprovable accusations would distress the old woman unpardonably. No. There was nothing at all she could do about it. She wasn't even going to be allowed to stay long enough in the house to look for proof which probably didn't exist.

Next morning she only had Emily to face at breakfast, and that was hard enough. She exchanged an affectionate farewell with her, promising to write and not to lose contact, agreeing with her about her 'inconsiderate boss' in London, and accepting her gratitude for all her work with a deepening sense of guilt.

Simon appeared in time to see her off the premises. It hurt to discover that his unexpected arrival could still make her heart lurch, despite what had happened. When they parted Emily didn't notice that, in the bustle of loading her car and exchanging hugs, her grandson and Holly managed not even to shake hands. In fact they barely looked at each other.

As she got into her car and drove off slowly down the gravelled drive, Holly couldn't help glancing in her mirror for a last glimpse of the house where her life and emotions had been thrown into such unanticipated turmoil. Simon was standing there, alone under the pillared entrance, hands in his pockets, watching her as she drove away. Like some avenging angel at the gates of Eden, she thought absurdly, dashing a persistent tear from her cheek, and forcing herself to concentrate on her driving.

CHAPTER SEVEN

HOLLY *never* wanted to be a lady of leisure. How on earth did people without jobs ever manage to fill their time? Of course, they probably had a whole network of friends who were similarly placed. Or they had children. Ruthlessly, she quelled that line of thought. Most people didn't spend as much time as she seemed to be doing in thinking gloomily about injustice or about the folly of letting your head rule your heart. Although she hadn't the faintest idea how she could have prevented that.

Perhaps she shouldn't blame her friends, who all had full-time jobs, for her isolation. She could be back in the warmth and love of her family with one phone call. She chose not to make it. For the first time in her life she was indulging in self-pity, almost wallowing in the misery of her situation. She spent hours thinking of Simon with alternating longing and resentment; she thought about his grandmother with affection; about Pamela she tried not to think at all. It hurt too much to realise how quickly and easily Simon had been led by that woman's plans into believing the worst of her.

Of course, it couldn't last. After four days of inactivity she began on the programme of cleaning and decorating which she had had to put off when the Danfield Court project had first come up.

She came downstairs late one morning to find a large brown envelope on her mat. As she turned it over something tightened in her stomach. She had seen that decisive black scrawl often enough in the past four months. She held it tightly, staring at it, reading the familiar postmark, and wondering what message it held for her. Almost reluctantly, she picked up a knife to slit it open.

There was no message. Not a single personal comment. Just the familiar sheets of paper which were all part of the routine administration of the Court. She remembered that he had said he would send them to her. She could 'earn her keep' now. She dropped the papers on the table. She'd do the work; do it so well that not even Simon Drayton would be able to find a single thing to criticise. But not this morning. Later.

She did get round to the paperwork later that day and, without the constant interruptions she had grown used to at the Court, it didn't take long. Not even when she had double and triple-checked every conceivable detail. She put the envelope back in the post without a covering letter.

After that, a sort of routine developed. Holly would receive an envelope every four or five days, complete the enclosed work, and return it. If it weren't for the distinctive writing on the address label, the whole transaction could have been completely anonymous. She sometimes had visions of life at Danfield Court proceeding almost as quietly as this uncommunicative exchange of business.

Emily had her grandson back in residence, taking on his responsibilities as the owner of the Court. It was, Holly had always suspected, what had lain behind that first impulse to open the house. His grandmother had known Simon too well to think he would allow any such thing to happen without his direct supervision. Once he had grown used to being home again, Emily had probably not been surprised when he'd rediscovered ties he could not break, and did not want to.

Pamela, too, was presumably satisfied with the way things had turned out. She had managed to get rid of

Holly, and now she had every opportunity to fix her interest with Simon, who hadn't yet shown any real objection to such a suitable, if cold-blooded, arrangement.

Holly didn't want to think about how Simon was feeling. Glad to be proved right about her? It wasn't a comfortable thought. She found herself scanning the paper every morning, only able to concentrate on other things once she'd confirmed that his engagement had not yet been announced.

Emily had phoned a couple of times, but the conversations had been constrained. Holly had not been able to bring herself to ask about Simon, and she was too conscious of the real reason behind her departure from the house to be comfortable with Emily's belief that she was now engaged on another job elsewhere. Answering kindly probing questions proved increasingly hard and she had not returned the calls. She hoped that her rudeness might hurt the old lady less in the end than discovering that she had been deceived.

At least this morning had brought a cheerful family letter as well as the usual heavy brown envelope. Jenny, it seemed, was temporarily heart-whole but about to spend a week on a cycling holiday in France with several student friends. Including one who 'might be promising'. With a sigh of envy for her sister's light-heartedness, Holly folded the letter to re-read it later. Perhaps it would have been better if she had learned to approach romance as lightly as Jenny did, she concluded ruefully.

Early September was still hot and sticky, and London seemed to trap the still air. The decorating was done and the work from the Court did little to occupy Holly's time. She was glad that in a few weeks from now this farce would be over and she could go back to work properly and forget the whole Drayton family. Who was she fooling? she thought irritably, and went to answer whatever idiot was ringing the doorbell with such peremptory insistence.

She flung it open. 'Yes?' she demanded, then just stood there, staring.

Simon glared back. 'Well? Can I come in?'

She stepped back automatically, and he brushed past her and into the small living-room. Immediately her compact flat felt cramped and confined. She shut the door carefully before turning to face him. He was looking around as though he had a genuine interest in where she lived; then his glance fell on her again and she saw his lips tighten.

'Have you been ill?' he asked sharply.

Holly was acutely aware of recent weight-loss and dark shadows bruising the delicate skin beneath her eyes. 'No, of course not,' she denied. Why did he have to look as vital as ever? 'Why? Haven't I been doing my work well enough?' She *knew* she hadn't left any room for criticism. If he was going to——'

Apparently he wasn't. He ran a hand through his dark, wiry hair in an uncharacteristically weary gesture. 'No, it's not that. Look—can I sit down?'

She had the feeling that he would rather pace the room, but there wasn't space for more than a couple of his long strides in any direction.

'Of course.' Uncertainly, she sat in her favourite armchair, tucking her feet beneath her defensively. Her delicate two-seater sofa barely seemed large enough for him, and she couldn't control her own response to his nearness and the confused and conflicting sensations she felt at his presence in her living-room. 'What *is* the problem, then?' she asked, realising that, for all his usual appearance of strength and vitality, he too was showing signs of strain.

He hesitated, looking down at the hands clasped

loosely between his knees for a long moment before looking back at her. She wondered, nervously, what he was going to say. When he looked up at her and spoke, however, he stunned her.

'Would you be willing to come back to the Court?' he asked simply.

She could tell nothing from his voice. It wasn't a plea or a request, more like a detached observer seeking information and not caring much about the answer. Holly thought of the past few weeks, of the accusations he had made, and felt a saving touch of anger after the first instinctive leap of delight.

'I can't think of any good reason why I should,' she told him. 'Can you?'

The faintest hint of humour touched the set severity of his mouth. 'Probably not. Although you do still work for me, don't you?'

'You had my letters,' she reminded him frostily.

'Letters?' he queried. 'If I hadn't recognised the writing I'd never have known who'd done the work.'

'I only followed your example,' she pointed out sweetly.

She caught the brief glint of a smile as he acknowledged the hit. Then this expression was serious again. 'I'm not asking you to come back for my sake,' he told her bluntly. Of course. It had been stupid of her to hope any such thing for even a second. He was probably hating to be here.

'So why are you here?' She spoke her thought aloud.

'It's Grandma.' His voice was heavy and she was at once alarmed.

'Why? What's wrong? Is she all right?' Concern, and guilt for the unreturned phone calls, swamped her anger with Simon.

For a moment she saw his hands tighten on each other. The quickly suppressed movement, more than what he said, betrayed his anxiety. 'No, she's not all right,' he said bluntly. 'She's tired and ill and beginning to realise she's not immortal.'

Holly wondered if Simon, too, had just begun to realise that.

'The doctor has ordered her to bed and told her that what she needs is rest. But she's worrying too much about the blasted house, and thinks the system will fall apart if she doesn't keep her eye on it.' He looked at her with a humourless smile. 'I did point out that you weren't the sort of person who set up systems which fell apart, but even that didn't seem to work. She trusts you, you know,' he added derisively.

Holly didn't know whether to be more touched by Emily's faith or angered by Simon's lack of it. 'Why don't you just shut the house early?' she wondered. 'The public will understand if you give a reason, and the season's got little more than a month to run anyway.' She didn't like to think of Emily at the Court lying bed-bound and restless.

'You think I haven't tried that one?' he asked drily.

Of course he had. It would have been the perfect excuse never to open his house up again.

He was shaking his head. 'She won't have it. It seems that the only thing that will make her stay in bed and relax is to know that you're back in charge. What about it?' he ended curtly.

How he must hate having to ask, she realised. He must have looked desperately at every possible alternative before his very genuine love for his grandmother had driven him to seek her out here. And she realised at the same time that she couldn't refuse. She would be doing it as much for Emily as for Simon, she reminded herself, and she didn't have to give in at once. She tried to school her face to indifference as she met his brooding gaze.

'And what do you feel about it?' she couldn't help asking.

He shrugged. 'What do you think?' His voice was neutral, unreadable, but of course she knew the answer anyway. She must be an idiot to *invite* insult. He went on before she could respond, 'Of course, I would make it worth your while if you did decide to return.'

That did it. A wonderful, saving surge of anger caught her and she stood up. 'You can take your money and do what you like with it. You can even keep your precious salary, if it's worrying you. I'll come back to Danfield because I like Emily and I don't want her to make herself ill with worry. Even if that means I have to put up with her grandson too,' she found herself finishing, glaring at him in fury, half appalled and half exhilarated by her own outburst. He's going to wipe me out, she realised, horrified.

Amazingly, he threw his head back and laughed aloud. Not the sneering smile which was all she had recently seen, but the honest mirth which had delighted her when she'd first seen him. Bewildered, she stood her ground, slowly unclenching her fists as she realised that he was genuinely amused by her reaction.

Something like real warmth touched his face when he spoke again, and she sensed that somehow much of the tension had drained from him. 'Thank you,' he said, 'on Emily's behalf, anyway. Can you come back with me today?' he added.

'Today?' she was startled. 'Is it that urgent?' Fear for Emily suddenly clutched her.

He smiled wryly, disarming her fear. 'Not exactly. It's just that she made it all too clear that I'd better not cross my own threshold again without you.'

Fascinated, she wondered, 'What would you have done if I'd refused?'

'Kidnapped you, probably.' Dark eyes scanned her

comprehensively, and Holly felt her skin warm. 'You look tiny enough to go in the boot of my car with no trouble at all.'

She wasn't wholly convinced he was joking. 'All right,' she agreed, knowing she had never had any choice, 'I'll drive up this afternoon.'

'I'll drive you now,' he said. It sounded almost like an order. She raised her eyebrows. 'You can get your car some other time, or use the spare car at the Court while you're there. At the moment you look too tired to drive any distance safely,' he added bluntly, 'and I don't want to find myself with another invalid on my hands.'

Holly gave in without a struggle. She hadn't been looking forward to the drive, anyway. 'All right,' she conceded. 'I'll need an hour to pack and leave the flat clear. Why don't you call back after lunch?'

He shook his head. 'I'll leave you to pack, but we can eat on the way.' He stood up, stretching as though relieved of a burden, and glanced at the expensive watch on one wrist. 'I'll see you in an hour,' he confirmed without giving her a chance to argue.

Why hadn't she said two hours? At least. She had hardly given herself time to change and pack a small suitcase before he was back again, the sound of his horn outside reminding her that he was in a hurry.

She slid into the cushioned luxury of his car's front seat. He might be the sort of person who *needed* a car of this size if he was going to be comfortable, but it must be nice to be able to afford it.

He looked sideways at her. 'I'm glad you didn't offer *me* a lift. That car of yours wasn't built for people of my size.'

She'd assumed he was in a hurry, and had braced herself for a fast drive. He didn't, however, push the powerful car beyond the legal limits and, after about forty-five minutes, he pulled off the motorway on to a minor road she'd never taken.

'Where are we going?' she asked. Stupid memories of his talk of kidnapping suddenly surfaced.

Simon laughed. 'Afraid that I'm going to murder you and hide your body in some wilderness?' he mocked her.

She looked out of the side window at the passing countryside and tried to seem indifferent.

'Believe me,' he added, a bitter note beneath the humour, 'I have been tempted.'

It did not take psychic powers to follow his thoughts back to their last encounter at Danfield Court. Then he shrugged off the darker mood as he swung the car into the drive of a sprawling stone building with a small sign outside. 'But I'm afraid this is simply a lunch-break.'

He must have phoned earlier for reservations. This was not the sort of place which catered for the casual passing trade. Besides, he was obviously known here. He was greeted by name and they were ushered at once to a table for two.

The business of ordering covered the first few minutes, but Holly was too aware of her companion to feel at ease. She looked around at the discreet opulence of their surroundings, even less comfortable as she realised that she was dressed far less formally than most of the other diners.

'We could have stopped at the motorway service station,' she said into the awkward silence which was growing between them. 'This is rather splendid.'

Their surroundings weren't intimidating Simon at all. 'Don't you like it here?'

She glanced down at the exquisitely presented plate of food which had just been placed in front of her.

'How could I not? It's lovely.' Then, 'Just how ill is Emily? She's not in hospital, is she?'

Simon shook his head, a quick frown troubling his face. 'No. To be honest, I don't know how serious it is—but it's not like her to give in to anything. The doctor hasn't found anything specific but, at her age, she shouldn't overdo things. She seems to have lost all her energy,' he added, not trying to hide his concern.

Holly could understand it. Emily had always seemed to have the energy and enthusiasm of someone half her age. 'I'm sorry,' she said quietly. 'Of course I'll do whatever I can to help.'

He looked at her, his dark eyes suddenly bleak. 'It's a pity you didn't act a bit more responsibly a few weeks ago,' he said with sudden bitterness. 'If it hadn't been for you she might never have got into this state.'

The unexpected accusation hurt, and stung Holly to anger. 'If you'd bothered to find the truth behind what happened then, I would never have had to leave,' she told him coldly. 'The obvious explanation isn't always the right one, you know.'

He looked disillusioned, as though he was disappointed that she should still pretend to maintain her innocence. 'It usually is,' he pointed out. 'Besides, can you prove that Dave was lying?' For a moment she thought she detected a note of eagerness, as though he wanted her to say yes. She must have imagined it.

Sadly she shook her head. 'No.' Because she was fairly certain Dave hadn't lied; but to accuse Pamela without a shred of evidence would be worse than hopeless. She wondered if even Emily's ill health would have been enough to allow her back into Danfield Court if she had gone on to say, But I think the girl you're going to marry engineered the whole business.

Simon looked for a moment as though he expected

more than the monosyllabic response. Another protestation of innocence, perhaps? He wasn't going to get it. He shrugged dismissively at her continued silence. 'You'll have to pardon me if I stick to my conclusions, then, won't you?'

She wasn't sure that she would, but there was no point in antagonising him any further. The rest of the meal passed almost in silence, and might as well have been in a fast-food place of some sort for all the pleasure it gave Holly.

Simon's mood showed no signs of improving as they neared the Court. He must feel as though he's deliberately inviting an enemy into his home, she realised, as the big car drew up outside the familiar steps. He came round to open her door while she was still fumbling with her seatbelt.

'Go straight in. I'll take the car round to the garage and bring your case in later.'

Not a word of welcome. What had she expected? It still felt oddly like coming home, though, as she stepped through the doorway into the wide hall. The housekeeper at least seemed pleased to see her, and directed her upstairs to Emily's room when Holly asked if she was up to receiving visitors.

In the four-poster bed, which must have held generations of the Drayton family, Emily looked shockingly frail propped against pillows. She seemed to be asleep as Holly opened the door quietly, but her eyes opened as Holly neared the bed, and an expression of surprise and pleasure lit up her face.

'Holly!' she exclaimed, reaching out her arms. The old bones felt fragile beneath her fingers, but Emily held her with unexpected strength. For a moment Holly rested her head against the lavender-scented shoulder, aware of tears welling perilously close to the surface.

Then she sat back to look at the woman who had somehow become so dear to her.

'What have you been up to?' she demanded. 'Simon tells me you've had everyone running round in small circles and worried stiff.'

A smile that could only be called mischievous touched the lined face.

'It won't do them any harm, dear,' she said placidly.

Holly wondered if they were both thinking of Simon.

Emily went on, 'I'm very glad to see you back, you know. I mentioned it to Simon, but he wasn't at all sure he'd be able to persuade your London boss to let you go.'

If Simon was to be believed, she'd done a great deal more than 'mention' Holly's return. It was ironic that it was he who had known quite well that her firm didn't even need consulting. *He'd* been the only 'boss' to be persuaded—and she suspected that even Emily hadn't found that easy.

'Well, I'm here for the rest of the season,' she reassured the old woman. 'So you've no excuses now not to follow your doctor's orders and get some rest.'

'Yes, but I feel so *useless* just lying here.' Arthritic fingers plucked irritably at the cotton sheet as though resenting their limitations.

Holly sympathised. It was no fun to be told to do nothing when you were used to bustling round and organising things. Her own recent taste of it had been more than enough.

'I don't know how long you've got to stay in bed,' she said slowly, the germ of an idea taking root, 'but it would really help if you could think up something special we could offer for the last weekend of the season. It would be fun to have some sort of celebration, and it would also make people remember the Court for next year. What do you think?'

A gleam kindled in the light blue eyes. 'I'm sure I can think of something, dear. Leave it to me.' A positive note had returned to the old voice and Holly stood up, satisfied.

'Gladly. I don't really like organising parties myself, and I know you can do it better. We haven't much time,' she reminded her.

'Don't worry about it.' It was Emily's turn to reassure her. Holly had the impression her mind was already busy with plans.

She was about to leave the room and think about resuming her own work when Simon came in. He strode quickly over to the bed and bent to kiss the papery cheek.

'Well, Grandma?' he challenged. 'Are you satisfied now?'

'Yes, thank you. It's nice to see Holly again, isn't it?' she asked cheerfully.

Simon shot Holly a sideways glance. 'Yes. Very,' he managed. He might have sounded more convincing, she thought.

'Thanks,' she muttered with equal enthusiasm.

As she left the room he called after her, 'I'll see you downstairs in a couple of minutes.'

The old gun-room was very much as she had left it. Had Simon worked here during her absence? The thought was oddly disturbing. Luckily she did not have long to think about it. Simon knocked and came in minutes after she had arrived.

'She's looking better,' he admitted. Hesitating, he added, 'Thank you for coming.'

And just how much had it cost him to say that? she wondered. 'I didn't have much choice,' she pointed out. 'There was some talk of kidnapping, and I decided that the front of your car would probably be more comfortable than the boot.'

His teeth showed in a quick grin. 'Grandma keeps reminding me how practical Capricorns are. By the way, what did you say to her that's got her plotting?'

She explained about the end-of-season party, and he grimaced. 'As long as I haven't got to dress up as a fortune-teller again, I suppose it's not a bad idea. At least everyone will be able to sleep in next day.'

He sounded quite cheerful, but the mention of fortune-tellers had reminded her too keenly of the day of the fête. She looked down at the tidy desk and fiddled unnecessarily with some pencils, conscious of his penetrating gaze.

'We never had that talk I mentioned, did we?' he said slowly.

Holly's hand tightened on the pencil. She could hear nothing but indifference in his voice and shook her head. 'No, but it's too late now, isn't it?' she reminded him.

'I suppose so.' She thought she caught an unfamiliar note in his voice but could read nothing in his shuttered face. When he spoke again his tone was businesslike. 'I haven't changed anything in your absence, so you won't have any trouble picking things up again.'

'Won't the rest of the staff be surprised to see me back?' she wondered. The housekeeper had seemed glad enough to see her, but she had braced herself for comment from the others.

Simon shook his head. 'No one knows why you left. I explained that there was a crisis at the London end of things.'

'Thank you.' He hadn't had to do that. He might only have been saving his own pride, but she was still grateful to be spared possible humiliation.

'Don't forget that I *do* know the real reason why you went,' he added savagely, as though suddenly angered, 'and I'm going to be watching every step you take.'

The pencil under her fingers nearly broke as she clenched her hands.

If she had her own car here; if it weren't for Emily upstairs. . .

'Then you're probably going to be very bored,' she said carefully. 'Do you want me to have an extra chair brought in here for you, or are you going to be content just to loom over my shoulder?'

To her surprise, he chuckled disconcertingly. 'You're so small, that looming doesn't take much effort. No, I won't need a chair. I'll just drop in from time to time.' There was nothing new in that, but then there wasn't anything new, either, in his lack of trust. He hadn't wanted her here in the first place, she remembered.

As he left Holly sat at the desk and wondered just how glad she was to be back. At first the opportunity to return to the Court had seemed like some divine reprieve, and she *was* happy to see Emily again and to be back in the house which had somehow enveloped her in its warmth and history. But she wasn't at all sure how well she was going to be able to cope with Simon's attitude.

If he was keeping an eye on her, he was doing it from a distance. She saw nothing of him at first as she went round the house, checking that all was well. As he had said, nothing had changed.

She wasn't really needed at all, she realised. Her work had been finished weeks ago and the house could run quite smoothly without her. She supposed she should feel pleased; it meant she'd done her job well. It was ironic that now, when she should be insisting that it was time for her to leave, she had no choice about staying on.

At least Pamela didn't seem to be around. Emily had said something about a visit to Paris, and Holly's only regret was that it seemed unlikely to last until the house closed for the season. She doubted whether the other woman knew of her return, and didn't look forward to hearing her reaction. It would be easier if they could somehow manage not to be alone together. Perhaps Simon was waiting until after the house was closed before they made any formal declarations of their engagement? Given Pamela's dislike of something she considered rather vulgarly commercial, it might not be so unlikely. At least she would be long gone before then.

Holly made her rounds of the grounds next morning. There were children chasing their way through the maze, but they didn't seem to be damaging anything. Older couples were wandering among the heady colours of the rose garden or commenting on the many varieties in the wide herbaceous border. She saw one woman glance round before furtively taking a cutting. This once, she decided to say nothing; in a way the petty vandalism was a compliment.

In the kitchen garden everything seemed to be flourishing, too. Small hard fruit on the trees espaliered against the brick wall promised a luscious harvest a month or so from now. But, of course, she wouldn't be here then.

As she walked across the close-mown grass, Holly glanced up towards the belvedere. There seemed to be quite a crowd up there. She decided that that was one spot on the estate she would rather not revisit just yet. But there was no way she could avoid the river.

There, too, people appeared to be enjoying themselves. The short queue for the boat seemed cheerful enough, and there were several families apparently content to feed the increasingly plump and friendly flock of ducks.

Behind her, Simon spoke. 'Keeping an eye on things?' he asked blandly.

The implied reminder that she had failed to do so before didn't escape her.

'Yes,' she said as coolly as she could, not turning to face him. As her eyes scanned the bustle around the returning river-boat, she noticed something that surprised her.

Simon must have seen her start. 'Yes,' he agreed, following the direction of her gaze. 'Dave's still working here.'

This time she did turn. Was he hoping to provoke her? There was a hint of challenge in his dark eyes.

'I see,' she said.

Her lack of expression seemed to irritate him. 'There isn't any reason why he shouldn't be,' he told her. 'He was a bit foolish, but he didn't do anything he hadn't checked out first. *He* didn't deserve to lose his job.'

The stress was unmistakable. She looked across towards Dave. He was helping out with some children, and seemed to be doing well. She thought of her hardening suspicions of Pamela, and turned back to Simon, managing, with an effort he would never appreciate, an apparently serene smile.

'No, of course not,' she agreed pleasantly, and took some pleasure in walking away from him, aware of the thoughtful frown which had replaced the scorn on his face.

CHAPTER EIGHT

THE sniping continued over the next week. If Simon's aim was to disconcert Holly and keep her uncertain of her response to him, he succeeded only too well. Several times she would have left the Court had it not been for Emily, who, although no longer confined to her bed, was still weak. Then, without explanation, Simon went away for two days. The relief was immense.

Had he just been any irritable or dissatisfied employer, Holly knew she could have coped quite well. Whoever had directly caused what happened on the river on that disastrous Sunday, she still felt a degree of responsibility, so she could accept some of his lingering anger about it. The pain she was feeling now was due almost entirely to the fact that business had become inextricably linked with her most personal life.

It was becoming increasingly difficult to bear the moments of scorn or rejection. He had turned coldly away from her only yesterday when she had said something which had, for some reason she didn't understand, provoked him. She had watched his retreating back and wondered whether this could really be the same man who had once held and kissed her with such passion. He seemed to have dismissed her from his life, and it would be so much easier if she, too, could find the key which locked such moments away beyond accidental discovery.

But she couldn't. Too often she found herself recalling those heady moments; it was almost as though some part of her memory clung to them as a shield against his current hostility. It was made worse because she had only to watch Simon with his grandmother, or helping the children in the playground, to know that it was only towards herself that he responded harshly.

Surely you couldn't go for long, caring for someone who despised you? Holly asked herself, her chin resting on her propped hands as she leaned against a window-sill one evening and stared out into the darkness. She almost wished she'd never seen the glories of Danfield Court—but that would mean never having known Simon. The odd lurch her heart gave at the idea answered her own question. Even in her thoughts, though, she found herself skirting around that dangerous word 'love'. And just who did she think she was fooling? She sighed.

'What all that about?' Emily's voice cut across Holly's gloomy thoughts.

She turned. At least the old lady seemed to be regaining some of her vitality, even if she did still tire easily.

'Nothing. I was just brooding,' she admitted.

Pale blue eyes focused more sharply. 'That's not like you, dear. You don't often mope about "nothing", I'm sure.'

Holly shrugged. This was one area where she certainly had no intention of getting involved in a discussion. Emily had a knack of making you confide things which you'd never intended to put into words.

The older woman frowned as she settled carefully into her chair. 'I suppose it's Simon,' she said resignedly, and Holly felt herself flinch. She hoped she had not made any obvious betraying movements, and eyed Emily cautiously.

'How do you mean?'

'It's obvious.'

Holly hoped not.

'He's finding it hard to admit that he was wrong and that you've made such a success of this season. Men like him don't always relish a girl like you doing so well, you know.'

If only that were true; they had managed to tolerate each other fairly well when she had been coping.

Emily smiled reassuringly. 'Never mind. I'm sure these occasional moods won't last.'

Occasional?

'He's very generous, so he's bound to admit the truth in the end.'

If he ever discovered it.

'In fact,' Emily confided, wholly unaware of the inner commentary which Holly could not control, 'I think something *is* bothering him. Perhaps it's to do with the London work he's given up. I know I never really thought he enjoyed it much, but perhaps he did—and Cancerians are good with money.'

She leaned back, apparently satisfied that the stars had everything under their control.

Holly rather envied Emily her faith. She was certain Simon had no regrets about the City job; he had his home, his grandmother's health was improving rapidly—and, of course, there was always Pamela. No, Simon Drayton was one person who was probably counting his blessings right now, and only waiting until she left his house to be completely happy. It wasn't a cheering thought.

Still, she couldn't let Emily see how she was feeling—and she was very conscious that she didn't know how safe those feelings were from Emily's acute observation. And she, surely, wouldn't approve of Holly's absurd infatuation with her grandson. She was as unsuitable as Pamela was perfect, and she ought to keep that well in mind.

They had been talking for about half an hour.

Tactfully, she changed the subject when she realised that there was someone else in the room.

Simon was standing in the doorway, leaning against its frame, hands deep in his pockets. It wasn't fair. He shouldn't be able to have this effect on her. No one should be able to make her pulses leap like that, despite knowing what he thought of her. He was, however, looking more relaxed than when she had last seen him and, though she waited for the familiar tightening of his expression when he met her gaze, it didn't come.

'I didn't mean to disturb you,' he said, coming into the room. He bent to kiss his grandmother's cheek, and then sat beside her, his size throwing her fragility into relief. The contrast was somehow protective rather than intimidating.

Holly sat quietly, listening to the conversation between Simon and his grandmother, preferring to remain in the background, but it wasn't long before Emily got slowly to her feet.

'I think I need some more of that rest the doctor keeps on about. No,' she insisted when both Simon and Holly stood up, 'I'll be fine. You finish your drinks.'

Holly sat down again nervously, glad that she could stare down into her glass to avoid what she might see in his face, although aware that if she hadn't had the glass she could have made an excuse and left the room. Now she was trapped.

'Why do you like this job?' he asked.

Had a truce been declared? She hoped so, and decided not to try to work out what had caused it.

'I love the historical connections and the contact with people.' She smiled reminiscently. 'If I had been able to take up my university place I think I'd still have wanted to end up in something like this—academic work would have been too dry. I might have taught, I suppose,' she added, considering it for the first time.

'You like children?'

Dangerous ground. Didn't he consider her responsible for two near-accidents to children? Besides, she had discovered that her imagination had taken his words personally and she was seeing a gangling young boy, all arms and legs, playing outside on the lawn, shrieking with laughter. His child. Theirs.

'Yes,' she admitted shortly, since he still seemed to be waiting for an answer. 'Don't you?'

He grinned. 'Usually. Although after a session in the playground I sometimes wonder. Where do they get all that energy?'

Her soft chuckle was sympathetic. 'Never mind. Only just over three weeks to go.'

'The summer's gone quickly.' The admission surprised her. He finished his drink, and she was uncomfortably aware that he seemed to be studying her. Was he about to remind her of what had gone wrong in the past few months? Apparently not. He stood up to refresh his glass, glancing over at her in invitation, but she shook her head. 'What are you going to do when this is all over?' he wondered as he splashed water into his drink.

All over? He had his back to her, and for a moment Holly could let her eyes linger on the broad shoulders narrowing down to his waist and those long, powerful legs. She didn't expect it would ever all be over; a glimpse of him, or someone who reminded her of him, even in the distance, would probably always set her nerves jangling and her pulses racing.

He half turned, brows lifted as though in query, and she remembered his question.

'I don't know. I haven't made any plans, but I'll probably go home to Yorkshire for a while. After that, it's up to the office; I'm a bit out of touch.' And not really interested in getting back in touch with what had once seemed such an exciting career.

'I'm sure you'll be busy again soon.'

Was that a dismissal of her role at Danfield Court, or reassurance that he would not pass on any reference to her assumed negligence?

She didn't understand this mood. It was gentler than anything she had experienced lately, and there didn't even seem to be any hidden traps. Gradually, however, she began to relax.

The evening was almost an echo of some of the companionable evenings they had spent together months ago. Almost. Then, however, Holly had not known what it was like to be held by him; the stream of physical passion had lain placid and undisturbed inside her. She might have wondered sometimes what it would be like to be in his arms, but she had not *known*. Now the current of awareness ran quickly in her, and the soft lighting and surrounding silence only conspired to focus on Simon sitting opposite her.

He was saying something about Emily and her plans, but Holly wasn't really listening. Her mind was lingering instead on the way his hands moved, the strength of his profile against the lamplight, the warm roughness of his voice. Her own gaze faltered and she stirred restlessly.

'Tired?' He spoke with a sympathy she didn't understand. 'You've been working hard.'

This couldn't go on. His kindness made no sense at all, but brought her perilously close to betraying herself. She seized the excuse and smothered a yawn.

'A little,' she admitted. Her body had never felt more alive, her very skin sensitive to his every movement. 'I think I need an early night.' She certainly needed to get away. She got to her feet. Simon rose, too, walking to open the door for her.

'Sleep well,' he said.

Holly turned to look up at him, sudden tears thickening her voice. 'Goodnight,' she muttered, but couldn't take the step which would carry her out of the room. His dark eyes held hers for a long moment, their expression unfathomable. He lifted a hand and she thought for a second that he was going to reach out towards her, but the hand fell back on his side, the gesture incomplete.

It seemed to break the spell. She turned away.

'Goodnight,' he murmured as she walked out into the hall, resisting the temptation to turn back to see if he was still watching her. She hadn't heard the door close.

She had lied when she'd pleaded tiredness, but when Holly did go to bed she found her body possessed of a curious lethargy. She moved with unconscious sensuality against the soft cotton of the sheets as she thought of Simon downstairs. Was he still lying back on the sofa, staring idly into the flowers which filled the empty hearth, or leaning forward slightly to listen to the quiet strains of music? She could almost see him—the small furrow of concentration on his forehead, the large hands clasped loosely in front of him. Holly stirred restlessly, allowing her thoughts the rare luxury of lingering on the past half-hour. Its absence of conflict, Simon's apparent warmth, the thread of understanding between them, made it an episode to remember. She didn't know what had caused it, and hardly dared hope that it would continue, but it made her realise the tension that she had been under since her return.

Until now. Stretching luxuriously, she drifted imperceptibly into a deep and dreamless sleep.

Perhaps it was a good thing she hadn't pinned too

much on those couple of hours, Holly later decided. Pamela came back from Paris the next day.

Actually, Holly gathered, she had returned home the day before, but she hadn't wasted much time there before arriving at the Court in her usual scatter of gravel.

As it happened, Holly was the only one around when she arrived. Emily seldom got up before midday yet, and Simon had driven into the local town for something. It was a Wednesday, so the house was closed to the public. Holly would have liked to have closed it to Pamela. Instead, she stood up and smiled politely when Pamela was shown into the small drawing-room where Holly was enjoying a coffee-break.

'Good morning.'

Pamela didn't seem to have time for social niceties. 'I heard you were back, but I didn't believe it. How on earth did you worm your way back in here?' she demanded.

Holly was taken aback by the speed and directness of an attack she had expected to be more subtle. Then she remembered that subtlety had never really formed part of Pamela's armoury.

'I was invited,' she said mildly. 'By Simon.' As long as the other woman didn't quite realise the circumstances involved, there was a certain satisfaction in saying that.

'I don't believe you! Simon would never have asked you back here after what you did!' Pamela's cheeks mottled an angry and unflattering red as she tried to find an adequate way to express her fury.

With a curious sense of freedom Holly realised that, after Simon's contempt, this woman's rage could not upset her. She even felt a vague pity alongside her own anger at the trick that had been played on her. She didn't even bother to throw the lie back at Pamela, contenting herself with saying, 'Ask Simon.'

Her coolness seemed to disconcert the other woman for a moment, but it didn't take long for her to recover her position. 'I don't care how you wangled your way back to the Court,' she snapped, leaving Holly unconvinced, 'but you can get ready to pack your bags again. You're not staying here!'

Short of repeating what she had already said, Holly could think of nothing useful to say. If Pamela only knew it, Simon was entirely on her side, but he would put up with Holly's presence while he had to. And he would soon make that clear to his fiancée. Holly had no doubt at all that she would receive her marching orders as soon as the house closed, but until then she was in the curious, and sometimes uncomfortable position of being protected by her enemy. Not that that made this ugly scene any more pleasant.

'I don't intend to stay,' she told Pamela with deliberate ambiguity. Then she added, 'Excuse me,' and walked out of the room.

She thought she had handled the scene quite well, but when she shut and locked the door of her office behind her she realised that her hands were shaking.

Pamela didn't pursue her to the gun-room, and the squeal of tyres could be heard minutes later. The gravel would need raking again, Holly realised, and wondered whether she ought also to ask the gardener to look for fragments of broken glass. The thought restored a definitely wilting sense of humour, and she unlocked the door. Why should she let that woman drive her to barricading herself into her own office?

Inevitably, reaction set in. Pamela's fury and dislike made last night's peace with Simon seem curiously far off and unreal. This was where his commitment lay, not in a temporary mood created by music and tiredness. Simon himself was fairly elusive that day. When he didn't join them for their evening meal, Holly assumed that he was out with Pamela, who was probably giving him a highly coloured account of that morning's scene, Holly thought sourly.

She couldn't decide whether she was right when she next met him. He was cool and preoccupied but, if the friendliness of the other evening had gone, the savage resentment did not seem to have returned in its place. He was detached when he spoke to her, but she had the feeling he was avoiding her company. Although at times she was convinced she felt his eyes lingering watchfully on her, he was always busily engaged with something else when she looked up.

And why shouldn't he be watching her? It was no more than he had threatened, after all. But somehow she no longer felt that she was under suspicion the whole time. She might not be proved innocent, but had he, for some reason, decided to reserve judgement?

Whatever his motives, his attitude made life easier. She even managed to stop avoiding Dave, something she had caught herself doing too often because she was afraid to see what he was thinking about her. It was both anti-climax and relief to discover that he apparently had no thoughts at all on the subject except that it had all been 'one of those idiotic mix-ups', and a deep thankfulness that his own job was secure.

She had been talking to him one afternoon as he cleaned the boat at the end of the day when she felt that by now familiar prickle of awareness at the back of her neck. She looked up. Sure enough, Simon was approaching.

He looked slightly surprised to see her talking to Dave, but only said, 'Checking security?' as they met.

The irony, the reminder that he believed that whatever she was doing was too little, too late, was still there, but its biting edge seemed blunted. He sounded almost resigned, she thought, as she muttered agreement and passed him on her way back to the house. When she turned to look back he was in deep conversation with Dave, but she saw him raise his head and turn as though he had felt her pause. She couldn't see his expression from this distance, nor interpret the gesture he made as he turned back to the boatman. Besides, it would be foolish to assume he was discussing her.

As Holly looked at her calendar that night she was suddenly bleakly aware that her time was running out. In little more than three weeks it would be over, and she would have no excuse to stay. The house would return to its quietness, although now that Simon had come home, at least it would no longer be masterless, and whatever impression she had made would soon vanish. Simon would be glad; Emily might be sorry for a while, but perhaps she and Pamela would find some way of adapting to each other. Even if Simon did reopen the house next year, she wouldn't be one of its visitors.

But this year's season wasn't going to end without a celebration.

'I think we should have a ball,' Emily had decided. 'Not many houses have ballrooms these days, so why shouldn't those who do make use of them?'

There didn't seem to be an answer to that. 'Do you mean a public ball—selling tickets?' Holly asked cautiously, not quite sure how Simon was taking to the idea. He was listening quietly, but had said nothing so far.

'Yes—but only to people who've already been round the house on an open day,' Emily had decided. 'Then they wouldn't just come to gape and, in a way, they'd seem more genuinely our guests. Wouldn't they?' The question was clearly aimed at her grandson.

He raised both hands in mock surrender. 'Did I say anything?' he protested. 'Besides, you're right; this house was built for that sort of event, and it's been quite long enough. Even if——' he slid a glance at Holly '—this summer has had its moments.'

It seemed wiser to stay silent.

'Good.' Emily was clearly satisfied. 'It's to be a costume ball,' she added, as though mentioning a minor detail.

'What?' Even Simon sounded taken aback.

'Costume. You know—fancy dress.' Holly could see that Simon was about to reject the whole idea forcibly, but Emily continued before he could find the appropriate words. 'I want to base it on the costumes in the family portraits. After all, they cover many periods, and I'm sure everyone can find something there to suit them. You didn't think I was talking about *silly* costumes, did you, Simon?' she wondered guilelessly.

'Of course not, Grandma. The thought never entered my head,' he said, smoothly unconvincing, the gleam in his eye betraying his appreciation of her teasing. He glanced at Holly. 'I'm afraid you're going to have to arrange this. Can it be done?'

Holly had thought he might ask Pamela to do it. Grey eyes sparkling at the challenge, she smiled her delight at the whole idea. 'Of course it can. Emily and I will do it between us.'

She didn't need reminding that, though Emily might be involved, it was she who would have to do all the real work, but she appreciated his 'Thank you'. It sounded as though he meant it.

In the end, Emily would not let herself be left out, and Holly was grateful for all her ideas. She wrote the advertising, arranged tickets and caterers and staff, but the details which would make it seem a family event and raise it above the average public ball all came from Emily. They agreed they made a good team.

Pamela didn't. After discovering the plans, she had barely spoken to Holly, but she had a feeling that there had been a scene with Simon. She had certainly left the house in a hurry after spending some minutes alone with him in the library, and had hardly visited them since. It was too much, Holly supposed, to hope that she would stay away from the ball itself.

She turned up two days before it. This time she deliberately sought Holly out, pushing the office door carelessly shut behind her.

'So you think you've won, do you?' she demanded.

Genuinely puzzled, Holly shook her head. 'Won what?'

'Don't pretend! All this stuff——' the contemptuous gesture indicated all the paperwork for the ball with magnificent impatience '——doesn't fool me. You think Simon's forgotten the incident with the boat, don't you?'

Clearly not, if Pamela had any say in it. Suddenly still, Holly wondered exactly what the woman was up to now. Couldn't she wait for two days? Apparently not. 'No,' she said cautiously, 'but it's over now.'

'It won't be!' Pamela warned viciously. 'I want you out of here tomorrow. You're going up to London to fetch your costume, I hear. Well, if I were you, I wouldn't bother to come back!'

Emily must have mentioned that. No one else knew what she, at first reluctant to wear any costume, had chosen.

Pamela was still staring hostilely at her. Every line of her body was a barely concealed threat.

'Why not?' Holly was surprised at how unmoved she

felt. When the worst had already happened, and you had long ago been torn to shreds by an expert—who was going to leave your life in little more than two days' time—these rantings seemed almost unreal.

'If you don't stay away, you'll regret it. This ball is going to be the biggest event here for ages——' Holly supposed that was a compliment in a backhanded, accidental way '—and I want to be able to announce my engagement to Simon then. Without you around. You've managed to spoil everything else so far; you're not going to spoil this.'

Holly had no idea what she was talking about, but the thought of the festive occasion she and Emily had spent so many hours planning being turned into a platform for Pamela was bitter. She would infinitely prefer not to be there; she didn't think she could face that moment of gloating triumph, or having to congratulate Simon afterwards. But if Pamela had wanted to keep her away, she had chosen the wrong tactics. Holly had no intention of giving in to vague threats.

'And if I *am* around?' she wondered.

'If you are, you won't have a career left. I'll make sure of that. I'll tell your boss about that phone call Dave made to you, *and* I'll tell the papers. Simon was too soft.'

Soft? Holly nearly laughed, though she was suddenly feeling very grim indeed. The threat to her career was all too real. She didn't want to go to the dance, anyway; why shouldn't she stay away? *Run* away, an inner voice corrected. From blackmail? No.

'You can try,' she said as coldly as she could. 'But I'm not sure how far you'll get without Simon's support—and you might just persuade me to tell him who really took that phone call from Dave.' Her voice was quiet and steady.

A look of uncertainty flickered on Pamela's face,

and was gone. 'Nonsense. He'd never believe you. Besides, there's no proof.'

No, but the vacant sensation in Holly's stomach told her that she had never until now been really convinced of Pamela's guilt. She had not believed someone could act like that. Now she had what was almost a confession. And, whatever she had threatened, she knew she would do nothing about it. Even if she wouldn't let herself be driven away. She could only hope, improbably, that Pamela was bluffing. She shrugged.

'Think what you like. But I'm not leaving until after the dance.'

She was never sure what Pamela would have replied because someone knocked on the door and pushed it open. It was only then that Holly realised it had not been fully latched.

'Ah, there you are, Pamela,' said Simon. 'I was looking for you. Can you spare a moment?'

'Of course.' The sweet tone was for Simon; the triumphant glance for Holly. 'Right away?'

'If that's convenient,' he agreed smoothly. 'I'd like a quick word with Holly first. Shall I see you in the library?' He held the door as he spoke.

The look Pamela gave Holly as she left held a mixture of suspicion and warning, but Simon obviously didn't see it. He was briskly businesslike with her. 'Emily tells me you're going up to town tomorrow?'

'Yes, I'm collecting my costume,' she admitted.

He didn't seem interested. A preoccupied frown was knitting his brows and his voice was impatient. 'Do you want me to drive you?' he said.

The tone of that would have decided her answer even if she hadn't already made her plans. 'No, thanks. I'll go up by train and bring my car back.'

He considered this, and nodded. 'Why not stay overnight and come back on the morning of the dance?'

Was he trying to get rid of her? She began to shake her head.

'Arrangements not under control?' he wondered blandly.

They were. It really wouldn't hurt to be away for a night. It might even make Pamela think she had changed her mind—at least it would put off another confrontation. 'Perhaps I will stay up,' she decided thoughtfully. 'It's not such a bad idea, after all. Thanks.'

He looked searchingly at her. 'There's nothing at all to thank me for,' he said curtly, his voice unexpectedly harsh. She thought he was going to add something else, and was almost relieved when he said only, 'I must go. Pamela's waiting.'

The story of my life, thought Holly drearily, and began mechanically to straighten the papers on her desk.

CHAPTER NINE

THE train clattered its way into the busy London terminus. From there Holly went straight to the shop, run by a friend, from which she was hiring her costume. Despite her initial reluctance, she found herself nodding approval as she tried on the dress under her friend's instruction.

Simon had driven her to the station that morning. He had insisted on doing so even though he had not seemed particularly pleased at the idea. A constrained silence had filled the car for the short journey, broken only when he had asked, presumably from politeness rather than interest, 'Which of the portraits are you copying?'

'None,' she had admitted.

A sideways glance only revealed the set tightness of his mouth. The politeness was clearly only a veneer. At any moment, Holly thought uneasily, he's going to remind me that I'm the least welcome guest at this ball. She was glad to see the station entrance just ahead.

'None of the Drayton beauties to your taste?' he suggested. Evidently he thought her presumptuous.

There was only one Drayton to her taste. And he was hardly a beauty and, at the moment, was looking particularly grim.

'You'll see,' was all she was willing to say as the car drew up.

He might not have liked her attitude, but he insisted on coming into the station with her. His silent presence made her increasingly uncomfortable.

'Please don't wait,' she told him at last, when he continued to linger.

He hesitated, then nodded. 'You'll be back tomorrow?' he asked, almost as though he wasn't quite sure.

She hadn't known she had a choice. 'Yes, of course.' Or had the question been a hint? Perhaps Pamela had managed to convince him that it would be better if she *didn't* come back? Too late now to change her mind. He had nodded curtly and turned away without another word. She watched him stride towards the car, half tempted to run after him and stop him and ask what was wrong. But, of course, she knew only too well how much he resented her presence, and, anyway, the station loudspeaker was squawking about the imminent arrival of the London train.

Several hours later, looking at the plain skirts of the dress she had chosen, Holly decided she had at least made the right choice. She had considered the many family portraits which she now knew so well. Some of the women, a large proportion of them in fact, certainly had been beauties—or had sat to very tactful artists. No, this was a better idea.

The costume was carefully packed up in its own suitcase, and Holly made the familiar journey across town to her own home.

She had thought that a day spent back in her flat, away from every connection with Danfield Court, would be a relief from strain. It wouldn't be long before this would again be her permanent residence, and she would have to try to rekindle the enthusiasm for her career which had so recently begun to fade. Unfortunately, however, even her flat wasn't free from Simon's presence. His brief visit, to summon her back to the Court, had left its mark.

He had been there for less than an hour, but she

could still see him vividly, dominating her living-room. She half expected to hear his voice demanding her return or accusing her of lying and incompetence. Holly shut her eyes in a moment of despair. She must be mad even to contemplate going back to the house to endure Pamela's night of triumph and whatever Simon might have to say to her before he saw her off the premises for the last time.

Nevertheless, as she drove west the next morning, Holly found herself hurrying, pressing her little car to achieve a higher speed than usual. As she passed the junction where Simon had turned off to the restaurant, however, her hands tightened on the wheel and the car's speed faltered for a second. Apart from that momentary hesitation, though, she completed the journey more quickly than she had ever done. She did not bother to stop for lunch at a service station.

The house was alive with controlled bustle. Caterers had taken over the kitchen, flowers were being arranged in all the state rooms and, high on a ladder, two of the staff were re-hanging the newly cleaned chandelier. Holly was caught up at once in the sea of activity, and quickly realised that, despite the apparent confusion, everyone knew exactly what he or she was doing. There was plenty left for her to get on with, but there didn't seem to have been any crises yet.

She went upstairs and took the costume from its suitcase. The few creases would hang out before tonight. Then she sought out Emily to discover exactly what still needed to be done. On the journey back here she had decided that, despite everything, she was going to make sure that the last event she arranged for Danfield Court was going to be a success. *She* was not going to slink away in disgrace, however some people might expect her to behave.

The day's only problem, in fact, was persuading

Emily not to do too much. The old lady's spirit seemed to have revived almost miraculously over the past few days. Today, she seemed to be everywhere. She was undoubtedly enjoying herself, but Holly was very aware of her recent weakness and determined that she should not tire herself.

Simon, too, seemed to have had a similar idea. As Holly was saying, 'Look, it's all under control—you can see that. Why don't you take a couple of hours off and then do a final check of everything this evening before the guests arrive?' he came up to them.

'Holly's right, you know,' he insisted in that deep voice. 'There's no point in knocking yourself out now. Or don't you want to enjoy the ball itself?'

'Of course I do!' Emily protested. She looked from Simon to Holly and back again before reluctantly giving in. 'All right. I'll go and *rest*.' She spoke the word with scorn. 'But it's about time you and that wretched doctor realised that there's nothing wrong with me.'

She turned and stalked off. Simon turned to Holly, a wry twist to his lips and a hint of conspiratorial laughter in his eyes. He was about to say something when they both saw Emily turn away from the staircase as though about to make some adjustment to one of the flower arrangements.

'Grandma!' he called sharply. With a brief sigh of exasperation he muttered something under his breath and moved rapidly in her direction.

Holly watched, chuckling inwardly, as she saw him escort her upstairs, speaking urgently and impatiently. At the top he looked back over his shoulder and saw her observing them. Something in his face arrested her attention and she took a half-step towards him before she saw Emily tug his arm so that he had to continue to escort her to her room.

When he returned Holly had become deeply

absorbed in consultations with the caterers and a series of telephone calls to confirm that the band was on its way. A hint of tension in his posture as he waited gave her the feeling that he had come to some decision and wanted to speak to her privately. Soon.

It took only a moment's consideration to decide that she would much rather not speak to him. Whatever he wanted to say could not possibly be good news. It could therefore wait until tomorrow—which already promised to be depressing enough.

Normally, she probably wouldn't have been able to evade Simon if he was really determined to see her. Today, however, was different. Circumstances seemed to conspire to keep them apart. She glimpsed him frequently but he was always busy, although more than once he had looked up from what he was saying to catch her gaze. After the third such encounter, Holly made a point of keeping herself occupied, preferably in plenty of company.

By the time she went upstairs to find Emily and see if she needed any help to dress, Holly had the feeling that Simon's temper was becoming distinctly frayed. She was glad she had managed to stay out of his way.

Emily, as efficient as ever, had organised her own help, and one of the staff was already there to help her to dress, amid some giggles and exclamations of approval. Holly had only to admire the splendid confection of silk and lace. Emily would look positively regal in the rich lavender-coloured crinoline.

Her own costume boasted no such grandeur, nor had she wanted it to. The choice of the Puritan girl's dress had been quite deliberate. She had no portrait among the Drayton ancestors, and purists would probably claim that she had never even existed. Holly didn't mind. From the moment she had heard the story, she had felt a curious kinship with the girl. Besides, surely even Pamela could not object to her wearing a costume as simple as this?

Thoughts of Pamela were an unpleasant reminder of what would probably be the highlight of the evening. It shadowed all Holly's pleasure in the ball, but she was damned if she would let it defeat her! She wouldn't give Pamela the victory of knowing how much it would hurt her. Carefully, she began to dress.

The heavily boned bodice, cut like a close-fitting jacket and narrowing to a point below her waist, fortunately fastened at the front. Had she had to lace herself into a corset, she, too, would have needed help. The lines of this, however, were simple, and emphasised the narrowness of her waist. The skirt, a dark charcoal-grey like the bodice, was plain and was given fullness mainly by the triple layer of petticoats beneath. The fabric flowed gracefully from waist to hem, rustling softly as Holly moved, drawing attention to her elegant carriage.

She regarded her reflection carefully as she finished. The slope of her shoulders was stressed by the wide white triangular-pointed collar, and deep white cuffs made her competent hands seem surprisingly fragile.

There was a small lace-trimmed cap, too. She drew her hair back, tucking it into the starched white linen. The effect was startling. Her grey eyes with their long dark lashes seemed somehow larger and brighter; the delicate bone-structure of her face was revealed, and the colour of her lips was heightened by their stark contrast with the monochrome costume. For a moment she had her doubts. Then she dismissed them. In contrast with the gay colours and elaborate costumes of the other guests, she would fade into the background. She might even be taken for one of the servants. And that would suit her admirably. She hadn't lied when she'd told Simon that she preferred to avoid the limelight.

She glanced at her watch before setting it aside on the dressing-table. Time to go down. Somewhere a clock was chiming and she could hear the occasional discordant note as the musicians tuned up.

Downstairs there was a muted bustle in the background, but Emily sailed serenely out of the drawing-room to greet her. In the wide crinoline she looked magnificent—and nothing like the dumpy figure who had given her name to the period.

'That really was a clever idea!' Emily's eyes lit up with pleasure as they took in Holly's appearance, making her feel both flattered and uncomfortable. Although the older woman had known of her choice, Holly had always suspected that she had had some reservations about it. They were apparently gone. 'You look quite charming. *And* you're going to stand out from all the rest as they try to outshine each other!' It sounded almost as though she was pleased at the prospect.

'I devoutly hope you're wrong,' Holly said with real feeling. A retreat into the wallpaper was far more in line with what she had intended.

She couldn't help wondering what costume Simon had chosen. He could effectively be anything from Tudor courtier to Victorian statesman. There were several impressive portraits which showed those family looks: the marked features and dark colouring went back for generations. So, she suspected, did the imposing presence.

Five minutes later her speculations were answered. With lace at his throat and wrists and a burgundy velvet coat over a white shirt, sashed with silk at his waist, Simon was every inch the Cavalier. A long sword hung at his side and, as he bowed over his grandmother's hand with elegant courtesy the long dark wig swung naturally over his shoulders. Holly caught her breath. The illusion was too perfect. When he turned to greet her, her only defence was to sink into a deep curtsy, head bowed, hoping he would take the gesture as mockery rather than the evasive action it really was. It gave her time to think, as well as a moment longer to avoid his gaze. She couldn't imagine what he was thinking—and didn't want to. Had she known what he would wear, she would have chosen any other costume but this.

'My mysterious legendary saviour, I assume?' he chuckled as she rose. 'I like it,' he said with what seemed miraculously like approval in the velvet-dark eyes which scrutinised every detail of her appearance from the cap on her hair to the soft kid slippers almost hidden by her full skirts. His warmth confused her almost as much as that thorough survey. Where was the impatient man she had been avoiding all afternoon?

Both Emily and Simon seemed to want to concentrate their comments on Holly's appearance. However flattering it might have been, she was deeply relieved when the first guests began to arrive.

Rather to her surprise, Pamela wasn't one of them. There had been no sign of her all day, but Holly had expected her to be one of the earliest guests at the ball. She had even half expected her to have been staying overnight at the Court, and had been relieved to discover that there were apparently no such plans.

Two hours later the ball was well under way, and Pamela had still not put in an appearance. When asked, Emily had not seemed very concerned, and Holly knew better than to think of asking Simon. And, after all, she didn't mind in the slightest. Everything, in fact, seemed to be going very well indeed. She had danced twice and refused several other invitations, generally managing just to exchange a few friendly words with a guest before slipping away to keep an unnecessary eye on the organisation behind the scenes.

Now she had a brief moment of solitude in which she could unobtrusively watch the dancers. It was a kaleidoscope. Bright colours, laughing faces, elaborate costumes—rich satins and velvets and taffetas, elegant lace, graceful fans and intricate jewellery—spun together. The rustle of silk and the swish of crinolines whispered through the music. Some people had come masked; some had powdered their hair. Beside her, a tall Cavalier paused.

'Satisfied?'

She nodded.

'You should be,' Simon agreed, joining her in her survey of the crowd. 'Grandma's in her element, and all's going well. Are you finding time to enjoy yourself?' he added, a little brusquely.

'Yes, of course.' She was, even though she was all too aware of the sands of her time here at the Court running out. And his presence beside her, his apparent goodwill, was a peculiar mixture of pleasure and pain.

'Good.' For a moment she thought he might be about to ask her to dance. But no. A tall woman in the lavishly embroidered and ornate dress of Charles II's reign had already approached him with a laughing challenge. He bowed politely and took her hand, leaving Holly to smile and shake her head at the plump little man in a Victorian frock-coat who had arrived with the other woman and was now, presumably because he had little choice, offering his hand.

Of course Simon was, in a way, as much on duty tonight as she was. Holly watched the laughing couple swing round to the music. Duty? The revealingly cut bodice and provocative smile were excuse enough for Simon's willingness to dance. And she was hardly surprised that he should be in demand. He wasn't handsome in any conventional way, but tonight he looked every inch the grandee. Somehow the lace and velvet only underlined the powerful masculinity of his height and build. His swarthy complexion gave an almost piratical glitter to his smile. No wonder his partner was looking entranced.

Abruptly, Holly decided that she would rather be busy elsewhere. In the next half-hour she glimpsed him once or twice in the distance, but he didn't approach her again. The ball was going well, she decided. Even better—if slightly puzzling—from her point of view because there still seemed to be no sign of Pamela.

Eventually Holly retreated into the now empty entrance hallway for a few minutes' respite from the noise and heat of the ballroom, glad that she wasn't burdened with as many yards of heavy velvet as some of the guests. A step behind made her turn. Simon was coming towards her, an expression she couldn't interpret on his face. Her hand crept up to her throat in a protective gesture, although there was nothing at all threatening in his approach.

'Holly? Have you got a moment?'

She looked around. Nothing, unfortunately, seemed to need her attention; besides, she couldn't go on retreating all evening, and she couldn't at the moment quite recall why it had seemed so urgent that she did so.

'Yes,' she admitted.

He gestured towards the library and, as they walked towards it, she caught a glimpse of them both in the big Venetian glass mirror on the wall: demure Puritan maiden with her dashing Cavalier escort. Simon must have seen it, too, because she saw the lips of his reflected image twitch in appreciation, although he said nothing.

He was just reaching out to open the dark oak door for her when there was a confused bustle of noise at the main entrance. Simon hesitated, looking down at Holly for a moment in a way which she found oddly disturbing, then glanced up and beyond her to the main doorway. She saw his expression harden, then he pushed the library door open.

'Wait in here. I'll have to deal with this.' He walked quickly past her, not looking back.

She didn't go into the library, waiting where she was until she could see what was happening. She didn't have to wait long. The late arrival was Pamela, magnificent in sapphire silk, and she was just about to throw her arms around Simon.

Quietly, Holly turned away from the library and ran upstairs, her soft slippers making no sound, only the whisper of her petticoats betraying her flight. And the dark head bent over the fair one in the hallway would not be interested, anyway.

She shut her bedroom door quietly behind her, leaning against it, breathing hard as though she had just run a race. The sound of the music from downstairs faded, leaving her in silent contemplation of her own despair. In some ways, nothing could be crueller than what had just happened. Earlier in the evening she had expected it, and would have coped. Now, when she had begun to believe that, for some miraculous reason, Pamela was not going to arrive, she had turned up and Simon had hurried to greet her. It wasn't fair. Just one last night, that was all she had wanted—and it had been too much to ask. In a few hours, at most, Simon would hold up his hand to stop the music. She could just see him reaching out to draw Pamela to his side so that they could announce their engagement to the applause of the whole county. And she would have to be there.

At the moment all Holly wanted to do was fling herself down on that inviting bed and let out all the grief and anger which was consuming her. But she wouldn't do that. In a few minutes she would wash her face and go back downstairs, and circulate and smile and pretend that nothing had altered.

She would have to do what she had always done: rely on her own resilience and a well-polished appearance of confidence to convince others that she was unruffled. Salvaging her pride might seem a petty consideration, but it was important when it was all you had left.

Or was it? Caught up in her own misery, was she in danger of allowing Simon to do something he would regret? If she really cared for him, didn't she owe it to him to do something about it? She remembered the day of the fête. She had decided then that nothing could be more destructive than the loveless marriage he was contemplating. She knew he hated dishonesty—wasn't that the reason he was bitter towards her?—but any marriage to Pamela would be based on lies. Not only the lies she had told to discredit Holly, but also the lies he would speak when he took his marriage vows. Holly wondered if he had yet realised how difficult they would be for him. It would be better for him not to marry, she realised with sudden and absolute certainty, than to marry Pamela. Surely, if she loved him, she should at least try to stop him.

In the end it was as simple as that. No inner struggle, no hesitation. She loved him. Even if he despised her. By the time tonight was over, whether she succeeded or not, he could only consider her more contemptible. But that hardly mattered. Not now. She would stand aside for another woman, if he loved her, but it was better that he remain loyal to Laura's shade than marry

Pamela out of some misplaced sense of family obligation.

She straightened, checking that the cap and dress were neat and tidy, the Puritan costume seeming more fitting than before. There was no outward evidence of her inner turmoil in her reflection, except possibly a slight paleness around her mouth. Her grey eyes were wider than ever. Smoothing the wide skirts of dress, she opened the door.

Downstairs nothing seemed to have changed, except that now the entrance hall was empty. In the ballroom the dancers were still active, although the crowd had thinned a little as couples wandered off to the supper-tables. There was no sign at all of Simon. She did glimpse one bright blue dress disappearing into the next room, but it turned out to belong to a rather pleasant woman who taught at the local school and was delighted to see Holly again and tell her how much she was enjoying the party. Of Pamela there was no sign.

Declining an invitation to join the teacher for supper, Holly went back into the other room. No, Simon definitely wasn't here. Perhaps he was already alone somewhere with Pamela. If he was, she was too late; there were limits to how far she would intrude.

'Oh, there you are, Holly. I've been looking for you!'

Not Simon. Emily.

'I had to go upstairs for a minute,' Holly excused herself. 'How are you? Are you enjoying yourself?'

The smile was still enthusiastic, but Holly thought she saw the beginnings of weariness in her face. Emily confirmed it. 'I'm having a lovely time, but I think I might go up before long.' She chuckled. 'I'm afraid my feet are beginning to hurt.'

'Dancing too hard?' Holly teased.

Emily's expression was distinctly impish. 'Let's just

say I've danced more tonight than I have in many years. Look, there's a chair over there. Shall we sit down?'

Fortunately, the chair in question could accommodate the crinoline.

'That's better,' Emily sighed. She looked at Holly, and reached out a hand to touch her. 'I know this isn't really the right time, dear, but I did want to tell you how much I appreciate all you've done.'

Holly wanted to speak, but Emily silenced her with a lifted hand. 'I think you know that I hoped Simon might come to terms with his place here some day. And he has. Far more than I dared hope.' She smiled half sadly. 'He even took a boat out sailing the other day.'

'But that's nothing to do with me!' Holly protested, touched by Emily's words. Her heartbeat had quickened slightly at the mention of the boat. Could she possibly have been wrong about how much Laura still haunted him? Never.

Emily was shaking her head at Holly's protest. 'Yes, it has. Only someone with your strength of character could have made this season a success. And it had to succeed if Simon was to realise how much he cared about the Court. I don't think it took him long,' she admitted. 'He's enjoyed this season much more than he'll ever say.'

'I'm glad you think it's gone well,' Holly said. 'I'll be sorry to leave.'

The pale eyes narrowed on her. 'Yes. Simon said something about your rushing off again. Can't you stay at least a few more days?'

Holly shook her head reluctantly. She had no wish to hurt Emily but, especially if she managed to speak to Simon, there would be no place for her at Danfield Court after tonight. 'No, I'm afraid I really must go back. There's work waiting for me in London, and I really do owe my family a visit.'

If Emily was quite clearly unimpressed by the demands of London, she seemed willing, if reluctant, to accept the call of family ties. A tiny yawn escaped her. 'Oh, dear. And when I think how I used to dance till dawn! Now,' she admitted wryly, 'my poor feet are full of complaints.'

'Why don't you slip away?' Holly suggested. 'I'll make your excuses if you like. People won't start to leave for ages yet.' She saw that Emily was about to object that she couldn't go to bed before her guests. 'Doctor's orders?' she reminded her. 'You're meant to rest when you feel tired—and, if dancing all night hasn't tired you out, then you're tougher than I am!'

'I doubt it, dear. You don't make a fuss, but somehow you seem to get things done.' She smothered another yawn. 'Capricorn, you know,' she added vaguely before deciding, 'I think I might go to bed after all. It wouldn't do me any good to be caught nodding off in a corner, would it?'

'None at all.' Holly held out her hand, helping the old lady gently to her feet, and walked with her to the foot of the stairs. 'Goodnight, Emily.'

'Goodnight, Holly.' A soft cheek gently brushed her own. 'You won't forget us entirely, will you?'

'I won't forget you at all. How could I?'

How, indeed? Holly felt the prickle of unshed tears as she watched the small, indomitable figure walk slowly up the stairs, the gallant crinoline swaying gently around her.

Turning back towards the ballroom, Holly smiled with affection for Emily. Her own family would like her. They might be from entirely different backgrounds, but the old lady had a quality which was almost impossible to dislike. Unless, she remembered, you were someone like Pamela. Perhaps that was because Emily had seen through the other woman's pretences long ago and, like her grandson, she had little time for dishonesty.

And that reminded her of why she had come back downstairs. Doubts were setting in. She was going to sound like a vindictive, petty rival, she realised. Simon would probably put anything she had to say down to jealousy or a desire for revenge—if he gave her the chance to say anything. And she was no longer so completely convinced of her own motives to be certain he would be wrong.

She was, she supposed, still on duty. Perhaps she should confirm that everything was still running smoothly before she resumed her personal mission. If she ever did.

In the cloakroom women were rearranging their elaborate costumes, trying to restore the intricate hairstyles which were beginning to collapse. The chatter was reassuring. It covered all the current gossip as well as comments on others' costumes and the ball itself. Holly checked the towel supply and other details while the buzz of conversation around her confirmed the ball's success.

'Fabulous evening,' one elaborately gowned woman was saying to her companion. 'They should make it an annual event.'

'Good idea,' agreed her friend, 'although I might come as something more modern, like a flapper, next time.' She twisted, uncomfortably. 'The hire company insisted on supplying a completely authentic outfit and this corset is *killing* me!'

Her friend nodded sympathetically. 'I know what you mean. But it does look super; it really does.'

Surveying herself in the mirror, the other woman nodded, pleased.

'You might be right. It's worth all the suffering—Peter was impressed, too.'

The giggles which accompanied this revelation suggested a friendly conspiracy which was going well. Satisfied, Holly slipped away. There really didn't seem to be anything for her to do here.

In the ballroom a waltz was being played. Although there was plenty of life left in the evening, its atmosphere was changing subtly. Some parties were becoming a little noisy, loud laughter over nothing much betraying their over-indulgence in champagne, but most people seemed to be increasingly absorbed in each other. After the initial greetings, the catching up on gossip, the discussion of the ball itself, and probably the speculation about Simon, the talk was becoming more personal and private. Couples were involved with each other, some dancing in their own silent world, some drifting off towards the terrace and lawns, others sitting long over the scattered remnants of supper before taking to the dance-floor again.

Of Pamela there was *still* no sign. Nor of Simon. And then Holly felt that unmistakable current of awareness, and looked up. He had just come in through the far door of the ballroom, and he was looking directly at her. Immediately, all thoughts of what she *ought* to do, all the carefully reasoned arguments for seeking him out with which she had convinced herself, vanished. Half tempted to turn and flee as she realised he was coming towards her, she could only stand helplessly watching him as he walked across the room.

People tried to stop him, joking comments and friendly hands asked him to join a variety of parties, but he seemed to reject them all with a quiet word or smile without once breaking his stride. There was something about the rakish Cavalier costume which made him seem more dangerously attractive than ever, and Holly knew, as he neared her, exactly why the Puritan girl had been fascinated enough to overcome all her fears and ignore all the conventional warnings of her upbringing.

Dark eyes glinted down at her. 'It's a success, you know,' he said, almost teasingly. 'There's no need to look worried.'

If she was showing signs of concern, they had nothing at all to do with the ball. Just how was she going to tell him about Pamela? How did one even begin to discuss any such thing? She must be mad. He looked almost amused by her silence. To break it, she found herself saying hurriedly, 'Emily's gone to bed. She was tired out, but didn't want to admit it.' Was that really her, babbling nervously like that?

Simon smiled gently. 'I know. I've just been up to see her. I don't think she's done herself any harm—in fact, she seems to have got back all her old enthusiasm. She sent me away to enjoy myself.' His smile widened into that familiar, captivating grin, and Holly's heartbeat quickened. 'It's about time you took the rest of the evening off, too. Or are you exhausted from fighting off all those queues of people longing to dance with you?'

'Hardly,' she heard herself reply. 'Puritans don't dance.'

Had she offered a deliberate challenge? She wasn't quite sure.

Simon didn't hesitate. 'I don't believe you. I'm quite certain my ancestor would have managed to persuade at least one Puritan girl of the delights of such innocent pastimes.' He swept her a courtly bow. 'May I have the pleasure of this dance?'

CHAPTER TEN

How could she refuse? Holly took the hand held out to her, and let Simon draw her on to the dance-floor. There should have been something incongruous about waltzing in seventeenth-century dress, but it didn't feel like that, and feeling was all she was capable of at the moment. He swung her round and their steps matched perfectly, despite the difference in their heights. For a long moment she allowed the spell to hold her. But she mustn't let it last.

'Simon. . .?' she asked, conscious of his nearness, the solid muscle beneath the velvet and the hand which held her waist. He looked down at her, a half-smile on his lips and a question in his eyes. 'I must talk to you,' she insisted.

The smile faded and his hand tightened on hers. 'And I need to speak to you,' he told her, a touch of grimness in his voice. Then he relaxed. 'But not now. Later.'

'But this is important,' she tried, her will weakening as he drew her closer.

'So is this,' he stressed, impatience and something less identifiable edging his voice. 'Business can wait.'

'But——' And then she gave up. She couldn't fight herself as well as him, and she, too, wanted to enjoy this moment. She could surely steal these few minutes of pleasure to balance against the pain that was in store? She would talk to him when the dance, and everything else, was all over. Holly abandoned herself to the music and Simon's arms around her.

Long minutes stretched out in a silence that was full

of underlying tensions but somehow not uncomfortable. If only, Holly wished dreamily, this could last forever.

It couldn't, of course. The music stopped too soon to a patter of polite applause. Simon held her for a moment longer before releasing her and stepping slightly away. With the distance came the first chill of reality. What now? Would he disappear to do his duty by someone else, or was the conversation she wasn't at all sure she wanted about to take place at last?

The music started up again. Holly saw Simon hesitate, then he reached out and drew her towards him.

'Simon——' Her instinctive protest died almost before it was spoken. And that marked the end of her common sense for some time to come. For as long as he wanted she would be the Puritan girl with stars in her eyes and an ache in her heart for the dashing Cavalier who was whirling her round and tempting her with a way of life that was so far removed from her own. Capable, sensible Holly Fielding could wait in the background for a little longer.

She couldn't even have said at what point they drifted out together through the french windows and on to the terrace. The music still played, muted now by distance, and they had only the clear dark blue of the autumn night sky for company. Until, inevitably, a burst of laughter heralded the appearance on to the terrace of several chattering couples.

Simon swore softly and Holly stepped back from him, blinking, as reality began to return and she remembered not only where she was, but when and who. Simon's voice was harsh, as though he was angered by the disturbance.

'Let's walk,' he suggested, indicating the steps down to the lawn, green-grey in the faint light.

The suggestion was more than half an order, and

Holly wondered if the inevitable was upon her at last. She nodded and turned to walk with him.

They didn't speak and, though they were walking together, they might have been yards apart. Those moments of intimacy on the dance-floor might, indeed, have belonged to a forgotten era. Then, at last, they reached the paved area in front of the maze, its dark hedges looming ominously.

Simon gestured towards the wooden bench, and Holly sat down, her skirts rustling for a moment before they were still. What light there was came from the glimmer of starshine. Beside her, Simon was more of a silhouette than someone clearly seen, a dark shape whose face was pale and indistinct.

'You look like a ghost,' he said quietly.

The last traces of the evening's magic still hung around her. 'Perhaps I am,' she murmured. 'Perhaps we both are.'

'Perhaps,' he agreed. And then, in a different voice altogether, 'In that case, perhaps I should follow my instincts and do what my distant ancestor would undoubtedly have done in the circumstances. And,' he added thoughtfully, reaching out to untie the lace which held her cap, 'what I have been wanting to do all evening.'

The cap slipped unnoticed from her head to lie, a pool of white, against the dark ground. She could, probably should, have resisted. But it didn't even cross Holly's mind. As his hands slid into her hair and tilted her head towards him, she yielded, moving closer and allowing her hands to slide up his arms to clasp his broad shoulders.

The first touch of his lips was gentle, coaxing, luring rather than urging her to tighten the embrace as one of his arms went round her waist and drew her closer. A tide of feeling—despair and longing and passion—surged in Holly and her lips parted beneath his.

At once the kiss deepened, his mouth slanting urgently across hers, demanding the response she did not, could not, hesitate to give. Wasn't this fantasy, not reality? She could respond as she had dreamed since those moments months ago on the belvedere.

Eventually he lifted his head and the embrace slackened, but only enough for him to look down into the pallor of her face.

'My ancestor had the right idea,' he muttered in a voice thickened by laughter and desire, and drew her close again. But the moment's respite had been enough to allow the world to return. Holly had again remembered who she was. Her hands against his shoulders halted him.

'Simon, no.' She stared up into his shadowed face, unable to read its expression. 'We have to talk.'

For a moment his hands tightened on her and she thought he was going to ignore her protest. Did something in her want him to? But then his arms released her, and she was free. In the warm, night air she shivered slightly.

'Yes.' His voice was curt. 'I suppose we must.'

Holly gazed down at her lap. Beneath the white cuffs her hands twisted together. Deliberately she stilled them, then stood up, unable to stay this close to Simon and say what she had to. Especially now.

'What did you want to talk about?' Behind her, Simon's voice betrayed nothing except mild interest. Had his pulse returned so rapidly to normal after those moments of starlit madness? Hers hadn't.

It was so hard to start. It could never have been easy, but now she knew for certain just how much personal feeling lay behind what she intended to say. Still not looking at him, her hands clenching on each other against the stuff of her skirt, she stared at the dark mass of the maze. Its paths were so much simpler than her own confusion.

'Holly?' The quiet voice demanded an answer.

Reluctantly, she turned. She hadn't heard him move, and she took an involuntary step backwards as she realised how close he was. He put out a hand as though to hold her, but let it fall back to his side before the gesture was complete.

'It's about Pamela,' she blurted out. Even in the darkness, she saw the sudden stillness which held him.

'What about her?' he demanded abruptly.

Whatever magic had been left in the evening was draining rapidly away.

'I wanted to tell you something,' she began defensively. 'Will you at least hear me out before you say anything?' She couldn't hope for more than that, and she held her breath as Simon seemed to hesitate.

'All right,' he conceded, after what felt like an endless pause. 'What were you going to tell me?'

Slowly, clumsily, because she felt that she sounded only as though she were making wild accusations in order to clear herself, Holly stumbled into the story of Pamela's behaviour. When she faltered, Simon just said curtly, 'Go on,' and she had to continue.

It sounded more improbable the more she said. She was glad of the darkness which hid his expression and into which she would be able to disappear once this was all over. At last she finished the story. A silence, which she feared she could interpret all too easily, fell.

When she had begun to think he might even just walk off in silent disgust, he said, 'Why are you telling me this?'

She couldn't see his expression, could hear nothing in his voice which would give her any guidance. She swallowed. Why couldn't he just go?

Surely it wouldn't take him much thought to work out her motives? But he insisted, quietly inflexible. 'Why, Holly?'

'Because you're going to marry her,' she said flatly. 'I know she's ideal for you in many ways, but at least you know my side of the story now.'

Now he could defend his fiancée in terms which would probably leave a scar.

But he didn't. 'Why does it matter to you who I marry?' he asked instead. He sounded curious, nothing more.

After all that suspense, her own anger was inevitable. Despite those recent minutes of tenderness, he cared so little for what she said that it was only of vaguely academic interest. He was completely unmoved. It was obviously none of her business. In that case he was welcome to stew in his own mistakes. She'd done what she had intended. Her skirts whispered irritably as she turned on her heel to walk away.

'Wait, Holly.' This time he did put a hand on her shoulder to detain her. Under its pressure she turned back, not wanting to. 'Had you forgotten that I said I had something to tell *you*?'

She *had* forgotten. She assumed he meant to confirm his engagement, and she had no wish at all to hear any such thing, but he had listened to her, and the hand on her shoulder held her still.

'Well?' she prompted.

He let her go. In the darkness she saw him shake his head slightly, and something which might have been the ghost of a chuckle escaped him.

'If you hadn't insisted on speaking first, I'd have told you this earlier,' he warned. 'I already knew about Pamela,' he said simply.

'What? How could you?' It didn't make sense.

'I was just about to come into your office to speak to

you two days ago when she was with you,' he explained. 'The door wasn't quite shut and you were arguing—she was, anyway. I heard her threaten you, and decided to listen before I interrupted,' he admitted. 'I got the whole truth out of her when we spoke in the library later on.'

'You *knew*!' Holly exclaimed. All her confusion and internal debate since then, the certainty that she had lost Simon and the probability that she would lose her job, had been wholly unnecessary. 'Why on earth didn't you tell me? Didn't you care?' Relief could come later, at the moment indignation was uppermost. 'And you even let me tell you all about it tonight!' she remembered.

'Yes.' She could hear the smile in his voice. 'I'm sorry about that.' He didn't sound it. 'I was just intrigued to hear what you were going to say.'

'Great. Now you know. *And* you've sprung your own little surprise. I think I'll go back to the house. The guests there might need me.'

His voice, quiet and unthreatening, stopped her. 'Don't go, Holly. *I* need you.'

Slowly she took a step back towards him. 'What do you mean?' She heard the suspicion in her own voice, but could not help it. Nor did she trust herself when she was so close to him. But she couldn't bring herself to walk away, either.

He reached out and took her hand. 'Come and sit down again,' he urged. 'I'll try to explain.'

Still half resisting, she let him pull her back towards the bench. Just how much was he laughing at her?

As they sat down he didn't release her hand but held it, staring down at it as though he really could read what was written there. His thumb gently traced the lines of her palm. Holly shivered and tried to pull away. Didn't he *know* what he was doing to her?

'I wanted to tell you when you got back from London,' he admitted. 'I almost said something before you went, but there didn't seem to be any time. It's hard to tell someone you've been hopelessly wrong about them, and grovel abjectly for forgiveness, when all the person is doing when you're trying to apologise is thinking about catching a train,' he added with rueful self-mockery.

Simon, *abject*? Holly couldn't even begin to imagine it. 'But when I came back. . .?' she wondered.

He let go of her hand to spread both of his own in a gesture of frustration. 'I couldn't get near you. Every time I thought I stood a chance of getting you on your own, you seemed to slide away or become involved in some urgent discussion with someone else. By the time this evening arrived, I was ready to murder someone,' he finished with remembered frustration.

Including herself? She remembered ironically how she had congratulated herself on her successful efforts to elude him.

'Then,' he went on, recapturing both her hands, 'I saw you in your costume for tonight, and realised exactly how my ancestor had felt.'

For a moment Holly felt the breath catch in her throat. Then reality crept in. She remembered how quickly he had believed the worst of her. His attitude had only changed when he'd known for certain that he had been wrong, and he had only discovered that by accident. Without that evidence, would he have believed a word of what she had told him tonight? She let her hands lie passively in his, but her tone must have told him of her withdrawal.

'I'm glad that at least you believe me now,' she said quietly. 'I didn't like the idea of leaving in disgrace,' she added with a light laugh which didn't quite work.

'I didn't like the idea of your leaving at all,' Simon

said softly, and then, before she could comment, 'Will you tell me now why it matters to you if I marry Pamela?'

Stung, Holly stared back at him. This time she did tug her hands away, standing up so that she could at least move away from him. 'Isn't it obvious?' she snapped. 'I knew she was lying.'

'And why should that worry you?' He hadn't moved, and his face was wholly in shadow, but he still sounded relaxed, and only mildly interested. 'I'm surprised you don't think we deserve each other,' he added.

'You probably do,' Holly found the energy to retort, 'but Emily doesn't like her.'

He chuckled appreciatively. 'That's the first time I've heard someone protecting the prospective grandmother-in-law,' he commented. 'I'm not sure she needs it.'

'More than you do,' she said pointedly.

'You may be right,' he agreed. He then added, more seriously, 'Holly, I really am sorry. I misjudged you, and I've no real excuse.'

She found she didn't like this sudden humility, even if he did owe her the apology. 'It's all right,' she said. 'It's over now.'

'Is it?' He stood up and came over to her. 'And what about what just happened?' he asked softly.

What indeed?

'Starlight and fancy-dress can create some odd illusions.' She tried to sound down-to-earth, practical. That was what she was, after all, wasn't it?

'Including the fact that you responded so sweetly?' He took a step clear. 'There was no starlight when I first kissed you.' His hand tilted her chin so that she had to look up at him. 'Did I imagine your reaction then? Even when I deserved nothing more than a slapped face?'

'Do you deserve it now?' Holly queried. She couldn't

move away; she wasn't sure how much longer her legs would support her, but she wasn't going to let him treat her feelings so carelessly. He bent his head as though to kiss her again. Faster than thought, her right hand flew up.

He intercepted the stinging blow before it reached its target, his fingers encircling her wrist and holding it still with no apparent effort. She struggled once against his iron grip, and then stood still.

'Too late,' he said harshly. 'You've had your chance.'

This time the kiss was as rough as the first one had been gentle. It was as though all the frustration of earlier that day had to be released in a moment of sheer male dominance before his mouth gentled on hers. When at last he lifted his head, Holly knew she could not have stood without the arm around her waist, holding her fast to him.

'I'm sorry.' He didn't sound it. 'Perhaps we really do have to talk,' he added in a different voice, giving her no chance to say no.

When he moved back to the bench it was with her in his arms, and it was his lap, not the hard wooden seat, that Holly found herself occupying. Curiously, all urge to struggle had gone, although the arm round her waist suggested he didn't yet realise it.

For a moment he toyed with her hair, then his free hand traced the line of her bodice. She caught her breath sharply at her body's reaction to the light touch.

'You have no idea at all how sexy you look like that, do you?' he wondered.

'Me?' Her astonishment was his answer.

'Yes, you. But we'll come back to that later.' Something about that promise made her relax against him yet further. *His* wandering hand might be intriguingly baffled by whalebone and lacing, but his cotton shirt offered *her* explorations no such barriers. She looped one around his neck beneath the surprisingly silky fall of his wig while her other tugged at the laces holding the neck of his shirt closed.

He put up a hand and covered hers. 'I can't concentrate if you do that,' he warned.

Her fingers stilled against him—for the moment. What he said next, though, effectively sobered her.

'For a start, whatever she may have told you, I have no intention of marrying Pamela. And I haven't had for some time,' he insisted drily.

Holly pulled away. 'You haven't? Since when?' Had all her worrying been pointless? He must have been laughing himself silly at her efforts to protect him.

He tugged her back against him. 'I don't really know,' he said slowly. 'But I suspect it started somewhere around the time I met a girl who didn't mind changing the wheel of her own car, and who didn't hesitate to stand up to me, even when she was trying to persuade me to give her a job.'

Holly smiled, relaxing again. This might not be so bad after all.

'I had intended to marry Pamela,' he admitted, his voice more serious.

'I know,' Holly said quietly. 'She was no threat to you, was she?'

His voice smiled. 'Unlike you.' Then he was serious again. 'After Laura, I wasn't sure that I wanted anything more to do with strong emotions. I wasn't even sure I could still feel them. And I certainly didn't want to take on that responsibility. Getting the house back on its financial feet was more than enough.'

'And you could do that at a distance,' Holly realised.

'I could until Grandma stepped in,' he conceded ruefully. He must have felt her start of surprise. 'Did you think I didn't know what she was doing? Why do you think I was so opposed to it?'

Holly nodded her understanding. She should have realised that not even Emily could manipulate Simon without his realising it.

Then he chuckled. 'Not that it's easy to get your own way when she seems to have a conspiracy going on with the stars,' he said ruefully. 'I even ended up reading that wretched book of hers.'

'Me, too,' Holly admitted. 'It didn't help much.'

'Oh, I don't know. It gave me a bit of hope when its opinion of you coincided so exactly with mine—and flatly contradicted all the evidence Pamela left lying around.' He gave her a slight shake. 'Why on *earth* didn't you defend yourself?'

'I didn't think you'd believe me,' she stated reluctantly. 'And there was Pamela. I thought you were going to marry her, so you were more likely to believe her than me.'

'Despite what happened at the fête?' There was definite exasperation in Simon's voice now. 'I suppose you decided I always kiss people I'm feeling annoyed with?' he mocked.

She shook her head. 'I didn't know. I'm afraid I don't know much about——'

His hold on her gentled. 'I know. I realised as soon as I'd kissed you. I thought I'd probably frightened you off permanently. You can't begin to imagine what I was saying to myself when I left you that day. It was when you came bursting into that tent, looking so utterly defenceless, that I realised things would have to change.

'But there was still Pamela,' he explained. 'We'd taken it for granted for months that we'd eventually marry—and I wasn't at all sure what she really felt. Oh, I knew the arrangement was as "convenient" for her as it was for me; we'd discussed it once, as if it were a business arrangement. . .' The shake of his head and the tone of his voice told her he could hardly believe his own behaviour. 'Then she became possessive and seemed jealous of you, and I thought perhaps. . .'

'That she'd fallen in love with you?' It wouldn't have been hard to understand if she had done.

'Something like that. From the row we had two days ago, though,' he added with evident relief, 'I feel fairly sure that it's only the house and the money she's regretting. Her brief appearance tonight was one last attempt to recover her position—even though I'd made it abundantly clear she wouldn't be welcome.'

Holly was far less sure. Pamela might not love Simon as she had come to understand the word, but she had a strong suspicion that the other woman had wanted Simon for more than his possessions. It would have been surprising if she hadn't. Some lingering sense of pity for her kept Holly silent. Pamela had been humiliated enough, and Holly had learnt all too recently how much that hurt.

'And now,' said Simon in a brisker voice, 'since you know I'm *not* going to marry her, are you going to tell me how you feel?'

'Relieved,' she said promptly, deliberately misunderstanding him.

She felt his infectious chuckle as he laughed aloud. 'Don't be evasive. Remember I can still sack you.'

'No, you can't. My job finished with the ball,' she pointed out.

'Which is still going on—and will do so until its host retires. And I'm not doing that until we've got everything cleared up.'

'Like what?' Holly wondered cautiously. He had told her about Pamela, and made no secret at all that he found her, Holly, desirable. But what did all that mean?

'Like the fact that I love you. . .' Simon's voice was quite serious '. . .and I want to marry you.'

'But you can't!' she protested. It was impossible, even if, somewhere inside her, joy was beginning to blossom. She didn't dare trust it. Not yet. 'You can't,' she repeated, almost wistfully.

'Why not?' The question was almost stern, as though he would take no argument.

'I'm not from your sort of background,' she tried to explain, not wanting to succeed in convincing him. 'I'm just——'

'Just you,' he interrupted firmly. 'You've got more personality than any woman I've ever known; you're lovely, even if you don't seem to know it; and you can manage a high-powered career under any pressure that's offered.'

Dazed by what he was saying, disbelieving, she managed a protest at that. 'Almost any pressure?' she qualified. 'I think you defeated me.'

'It's the other way round. Haven't you realised that yet?' he demanded, turning her face in his hand and snatching a brief, hard kiss.

'What I *don't* know,' he added, exasperation and tension mingling in his voice, 'is how *you* feel. You always look so damned controlled,' he finished with evident irritation.

Controlled? After the past weeks she had no control left! And she no longer needed it, she realised. Holly turned in Simon's arms so that she could touch her lips to his, teasing him with butterfly kisses until his hand behind her head held her still for a long, searching kiss which left her breathless and shaking when at last he slackened his embrace.

'Well?' he demanded, but the tension had gone from his voice, acknowledging that he had already had his reply in her ardent response.

Holly relaxed against him, her hands straying among the laces of his shirt. Even knowing he loved her, it was almost as hard as telling him about Pamela. But, when she began to speak, she discovered it was easy, after all.

'Yes, I love you. Yes, I'll marry you,' she said simply at last. And then found herself unable to speak for a very long time.

'Why did you believe Pamela at first?' Holly wondered aloud eventually, when she was capable of thinking anything. Most of the hurt had gone, but she still didn't like to think of that scene with him in her office.

She felt him wince. 'I must have been mad,' he admitted. He then went on, 'In some ways, I was. It was just that the accident could so easily have ended in someone's drowning, and that got tangled in my mind with my growing realisation that I loved you, but didn't know how you felt about me.'

'And there was Laura,' Holly remembered.

'Yes, there was Laura. When I heard Dave's story, I suppose I just went up in flames. I tore back to the office, furious and frightened—but I still somehow expected you to prove that it was all false. And when you didn't, . .' He hesitated.

'And when I didn't, you decided that perhaps it was my fault after all. No wonder you were bitter,' Holly said sadly.

'Perhaps. But Grandma will never know just how grateful I was to her for giving me an excuse to get you back. I didn't know what to believe by then—but I did know you belonged here.'

So Emily *hadn't* had to do more than mention it? The threats of banishment had been Simon's invention. Holly smiled in the darkness.

When he next spoke Simon's voice was serious.

'About Laura, Holly,' he began. She tensed. 'It was over a long time ago,' he said quietly. 'The trouble was that I didn't fully realise that until that day on the river when I began to see that it was your innocence which mattered more than anything else. There aren't going to be any ghosts in our marriage,' he promised, stilling a fear that had barely begun to form.

'Thank you,' she murmured, grateful for his understanding. 'You know,' she said smiling, 'I was dreading this evening. I nearly didn't come back.'

'I was afraid you wouldn't,' he admitted. 'I was quite prepared to come up to London to fetch you.'

If he had done, perhaps she would have been able to spare herself several hours of unnecessary torment. She should obey her impulses, rather than a sense of duty, more often.

'I thought you were going to announce your engagement tonight,' she told him. In the distance they could still faintly hear the sound of music coming from the house. Holly realised it couldn't be much after midnight.

Simon stood up, swinging her to her feet, his big hands almost spanning her waist. 'I am,' he decided. 'Come on.'

He put his arm round her as they walked slowly back up the lawn. There were advantages to being short. With his arm around her shoulders she could tuck in close to him, her own arm beneath the velvet of his coat, resting on the fine cotton of his shirt. She was very aware of the firmness of flesh and muscle beneath the single layer of cloth.

He seemed equally aware of her. Every few yards he stopped to kiss her again, as though, like her, he still found it hard to believe that this was real.

As she leaned, breathless, against him, she heard him chuckle.

'Tomorrow, you and I are going off alone together,' he decided, although she found nothing to protest against in his plans. 'All day. And we're going to be firmly back in the twentieth century. You have no idea,' he explained, a faint tremor of passion beneath the laughter in his words, 'how frustrating all this whalebone and petticoats is proving.'

Her own laugh was equally shaken, her body's demands increasingly clamorous. 'I think I've a very good idea,' she confessed. She had had no idea that you could actually *ache* with pleasure. His embrace tightened almost painfully, and her mouth was bruised beneath his. Then he let her go abruptly.

'Come on.' His voice was harsh and his breathing unsteady. But so was hers. He tugged her hand. 'Let's get this announcement over with, and break the news to Emily.'

A last flicker of uncertainty made Holly falter. 'Are you sure she'll approve?' she wondered.

That rich explosion of laughter which had enchanted her when she'd first heard it made Holly smile, and eased the tension building between them.

'Of course she will,' he told her firmly. 'She's been telling me how compatible our signs are since March. You surely don't think any of this is coincidence?' he teased. 'Come on.'

And there really was no answer to that. With a wide smile of her own, Holly allowed herself to be led into the house, towards what was obviously fore-ordained to be her destiny.

STARGAZING

YOUR STAR SIGN: **CAPRICORN**
(**December 23 – January 20**)

CAPRICORN is the tenth sign of the Zodiac, ruled by the planet Saturn and controlled by the element of Earth. These make you patient, prudent, reliable and—sometimes—selfish. Your need to be secure and in control and your high sense of achievement make you a natural climber of life, whose ultimate satisfaction is to fulfil a long-term goal—even if it is an uphill struggle!

Socially, Capricorns are reserved and selective in their choice of friends—but you do have a dry sense of humour and realise that fun and laughter can break down the barriers. At home, you like everything to be organised and carefully planned, though your strong sense of duty can be somewhat overbearing for those who live with you!

Your characteristics in love: Naturally shy and cautious at first, Capricorns are steady and careful in love and only when they feel more comfortable with partners do they reveal more of themselves. Nevertheless, you can make an excellent partner and your need for emotional security and permanency makes you very faithful and loyal in a relationship. For the Capricorn woman, relationships with the opposite sex can be tenuous because of your constant fear of rejection and getting hurt; being so vulnerable and fragile in love, you will give as good as you get. Therefore, you are likely to choose partners who will support you emotionally and boost your confidence sky-high!

Star signs which are compatible with you: Taurus, **Virgo**, **Scorpio**, and **Pisces** are the most harmonious, while **Cancer**, **Aries** and **Libra** provide you with a challenge. Partners born under other signs can be compatible, depending on which planets reside in their House of Personality and Romance.

What is your star-career? Work, for many Capricorns, is the greatest priority in life and, fired on with ambition and perseverance, they tend to have a definite and realistic goal at all times. Being kings of self-discipline and patience, positions which involve a high-level of responsibility and challenge will appeal to you, such as engineering, architecture, civil service, politics and surveying.

Your colours and birthstones: Capricorns tend to like subdued colours such as browns, greys and blacks to match their pessimistic nature.

Your birthstones are black jet and garnet; the latter gem comes in a variety of colours such as black, red, pink, orange or green and is known for its healing powers, especially for arthritis and, more recently, to aid couples without children emotionally and physically.

CAPRICORN ASTRO-FACTFILE

Day of the week: Saturday.
Countries: India, Mexico, Afghanistan and Bulgaria
Flowers: Carnation, camellia & black poppy
Food: Coconut and beetroot; Capricorns love simple but good quality food and have an up-to-date knowledge of the most fashionable restaurants in town and the 'right' products to store in their kitchen cupboards.
Health: Disciplined in a regime of fitness and health, Capricorns tend to be the most long-lasting signs under the Zodiac—but be careful with your tendency to worry as you don't want to make excessive demands on yourself!

You share your star sign with these famous names:

Faye Dunaway	Diane Keaton
Annie Lennox	David Bowie
Rowan Atkinson	Paul Young
Dolly Parton	Rod Stewart
Maggie Smith	Muhammad Ali

Mills & Boon

present

Sally Wentworth's 50th Romance

The Golden Greek

Sally Wentworth has been writing for Mills & Boon for nearly 14 years. Her books are sold worldwide and translated into many different languages.

The Golden Greek, her 50th best selling romance will be available in the shops from December 1991,
priced at £1.60.

Available from Boots, Martins, John Menzies, W.H. Smith and other paperback stockists.

Also available from Mills & Boon Reader Service, PO Box 236, Thornton Road, Croydon, Surrey, CR9 3RU

From the author of Mirrors comes an enchanting romance

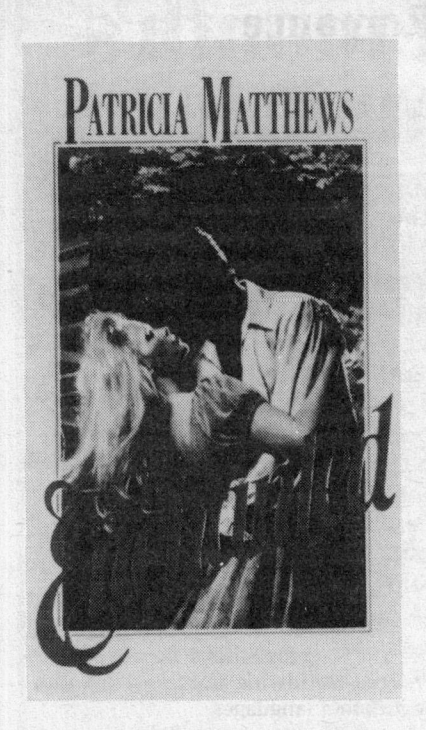

Caught in the steamy heat of America's New South, Rebecca Trenton finds herself torn between two brothers – she yearns for one, but a dark secret binds her to the other.

Off the coast of South Carolina lay Pirate's Bank – a small island as intriguing as the legendary family that lived there. As the mystery surrounding the island deepened, so Rebecca was drawn further into the family's dark secret – and only one man's love could save her from the treachery which now threatened her life.

W✪RLDWIDE

AVAILABLE IN JANUARY 1992 – PRICE: £3.99

Available from Boots, Martins, John Menzies, W.H. Smith, most supermarkets and other paperback stockists.
Also available from Mills & Boon Reader Service, PO Box 236, Thornton Road, Croydon, Surrey, CR9 3RU

Mills & Boon

Next month's Romances

Each month, you can choose from a world of variety in romance with Mills & Boon. These are the new titles to look out for next month.

DESPERATE MEASURES Sara Craven
STRANGER FROM THE PAST Penny Jordan
FATED ATTRACTION Carole Mortimer
A KIND OF MAGIC Betty Neels
A CANDLE FOR THE DEVIL Susanne McCarthy
TORRID CONFLICT Angela Wells
LAST SUMMER'S GIRL Elizabeth Barnes
DESERT DESTINY Sarah Holland
THE CORSICAN GAMBIT Sandra Marton
GAMES FOR SOPHISTICATES Diana Hamilton
SUBSTITUTE HUSBAND Margaret Callaghan
MIRROR IMAGE Melinda Cross
LOVE BY DESIGN Rosalie Ash
IN PURSUIT OF LOVE Jayne Bauling
NO LAST SONG Ann Charlton

STARSIGN
ENIGMA MAN Nicola West

Available from Boots, Martins, John Menzies, W.H. Smith, most supermarkets and other paperback stockists.

Also available from Mills and Boon Reader Service, P.O. Box 236, Thornton Road, Croydon, Surrey CR9 3RU.